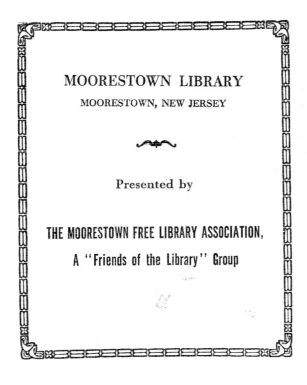

MOORESTOWN LIBRARY

MOORESTOWN, NEW JERSEY

Presented by

THE MOORESTOWN FREE LIBRARY ASSOCIATION,

A "Friends of the Library" Group

DEATH HAS A SMALL VOICE

Also by Frances and Richard Lockridge
in Thorndike Large Print

The Norths Meet Murder
Murder Is Served
Murder Within A Murder
The Dishonest Murderer
Death Takes A Bow

The Production Review Committee of N.A.V.H.
has found this book to meet its criteria
for large type publications.

Death Has a Small Voice

A Mr. and Mrs. North Mystery

FRANCES AND RICHARD LOCKRIDGE

Thorndike Press • Thorndike, Maine

Library of Congress Cataloging in Publication Data:

Lockridge, Frances Louise Davis.
   Death has a small voice : a Mr. and Mrs. North mystery
/ Frances and Richard Lockridge. -- Lg. print.
   p.   cm.
   ISBN 0-89621-991-7 (alk. paper : lg. print)
   1. Large type books. I. Lockridge, Richard, 1898-   .
II. Title.
[PS3523.O243D43 1990]   90-10809
813'.54--dc20   CIP

Thorndike Press Large Print edition published in 1990 by
arrangement with Harper & Row Publishers.

Cover design by James B. Murray.

**The trees indicium is a trade mark of Thorndike
Press.**

This book is printed on acid-free, high opacity paper. ∞

DEATH HAS A SMALL VOICE

I

He was a small, quick man, walking an unfamiliar street. He was pleased with himself. As he walked toward the subway, he hooked his thumb in the right hand pocket of his suit jacket and, with patting movements of his fingers, reassured himself that nothing had happened to the stiff, square envelope. Tomorrow evening, that envelope was going to be worth five thousand dollars. And there was no real reason things should stop with that.

They caved in when you really had it on them. Big shots and little shots, if you really had it on them, they caved in. All you needed was a break and he had had his. It had been a good while coming. Twenty-four hours ago — less than twenty-four hours ago — the break had seemed as far away as it had in all the thirty-odd years of his life. Now it was in his pocket, as good as money. He walked jauntily along the unfamiliar street — the quiet street, the dull street. A man could walk along it for blocks and not find a single bar.

7

Not that he particularly wanted a bar. He owed himself one, maybe two; he had something to celebrate. But there was no hurry. Perhaps he'd come across a bar when he got to Broadway; maybe he would wait until he got downtown again, and have a couple at Julio's. He'd run into somebody at Julio's. He might even stand a drink, although he wouldn't — you could lay odds he wouldn't — give anything away. This one wasn't going to be cut up.

Tall, dignified buildings were only a couple of blocks away as he walked toward Broadway. He could see them above the lower buildings. The smart guys hung out in them, the bright boys. That was what they thought. What they thought gave you a laugh. He did laugh, briefly. Big shots and little shots and bright boys, they caved in when you had it on them. Or even — and this was funnier even than that — when you made them think you had it on them.

That was the best thing about the whole unexpected deal. When he had started out the night before he had had no idea what he was going to happen on, and when he had made the telephone call this evening he wasn't really sure what he had. He had something that looked like being something — that was what it came to. A really bright boy might have talked him out of it.

And anybody could have talked him out of getting into the little house in the first place. He had almost talked himself out of it, because what would anybody who lived in a house like that have that would be worth the trouble? He had had to remind himself that people who have even tiny houses in the city of New York are likely to leave lying around things worth picking up. He had had to point out to himself how easy it was, with a rear window not quite closed. Of course, he was usually like that; jobs did make him nervous. Well, it would be a good long time, now, before he would have to work again. Maybe he'd never have to. Maybe he could quit with his luck good.

Even now, when it had turned out so well, thinking of last night made him feel jumpy. It had been a close one; there had been a couple of times when the best thing he could hope for had seemed to be that he would get out in one piece. That was the trouble with the racket; he could admit that now that he was getting out of it. You either got excited, like Sammy said he always did, or you just got nervous. He got nervous.

All the same, he would like to see Sammy in the spot he had been in last night when they came home at just the wrong time. He'd like to see Sammy running up and down those narrow stairs and hiding in the bathroom — and finding there wasn't any fire escape; a violation that was, if he'd ever heard of one — and then, when things looked like settling down, having this other one show up — the one she had greeted, in a funny voice, by name. Sammy would have been nervous all right; hell, Sammy would have been scared. Anybody would have been. He had been. If he had had a chance, he'd have cut the whole thing. If they hadn't been where they could see the door, and reach it in a couple of steps, he'd have run like — well, like a scared rabbit. Instead of which, he had had to get back to the bathroom, and hope neither of them would want to use it.

Even now, walking through the warm night, along the quiet street, he shivered involuntarily when he thought how close it had been — and what being caught would have meant. He breathed again the warm dampness of the bathroom; listened again for sounds which would mean he had a chance to get out of the little house. He heard again the raised voices from below, tried again — and failed again — to overhear words which would give him some inkling of what was planned. He heard the voices raised again, as if they were arguing, and then, once more, that long silence. The silence had been worse than anything.

What the silence meant he could guess at now; had guessed at. But then it could have

10

meant anything, and it told nothing. He had been forced merely to sweat it out — very literally to sweat it out, since the bathroom was hot, the air dripping. It had been odd to sweat and still be cold with nervousness; to sweat and shiver at the same moment. It had seemed an hour before he heard the outside door close.

And even then he had had to wait, of course. He'd like to see Sammy, cocky Sammy, sweating that out, waiting for someone to come up the stairs on the way to bed — and waiting. *And* waiting. And knowing that a bathroom is an almost inevitable stop-over on the way to bed. (Of course, Sammy wasn't a three-time loser; that made a difference, made it easier to be cocky.)

Well — it was over, now. He wasn't waiting there any longer, listening to nothing, waiting for a lead. He was walking down a quiet street with a six-inch-square envelope, five grand worth of envelope, in his right hand jacket pocket, his fingers tapping it. Nothing now to nerve himself up to, as he had nerved himself to leave the bathroom and have a shot at getting out. That had been the last tough thing; the rest was velvet. It was velvet that they were both gone, leaving the little house empty except for him. It was velvet that, finding nothing much else he wanted, he had taken the shiny little plastic machine, which was new looking and obviously worth a buck or two and, in its case, portable. It hadn't looked like velvet, merely like a buck or two — which proved that you couldn't tell. As soon as he heard —

He was midway of the last long, quiet block; the next street was Broadway. Even this far uptown you could tell it, the broad, bright street. The subway station was at the corner; trains ran through it toward the familiarity of downtown.

The station wagon passed him slowly, drew in to the curb ahead of him indifferently, without menace. But he knew, all the same. He knew before he saw who got out of the car, unmistakable even in the dim light.

The small man was quick. He turned back quickly, and thought quickly. He had just passed a mail box. That would fix it. He walked, then he ran, toward the box, and as he ran he tugged to get the envelope out of his jacket pocket. He heard running steps behind him.

All he had to do was to make the box. The box was sanctuary; if he reached the box he was safe on base, untouchable. He held out his left hand toward the iron box as he ran the last few steps; his fingers clutched at the iron tongue of the box, and pulled it toward him, pulled it down. His right hand with the envelope in it came up to the slot and then —

Then he was safe. He started to turn.

But then there was a great clanging — that was the mouth of the box clanging shut. That was —

His fingers had relaxed, by then. Then the noise stopped. There was no sound, then.

He did not really hear the clanging as the box closed on a six-by-six envelope. But the sound was heard.

II

She wasn't coming home to an empty apartment; that was one of the many things about having cats. Pamela North, trim in a fall coat, hatless, week-end bag in her left hand, could hear Gin through the door. One could hear Gin through almost anything. Pam put her key in the lock and all three spoke as the door opened. Gin spoke from the radio; Martini from the arm of a sofa; Sherry from the floor. They spoke with indignation, and Martini was the most indignant.

"Th' Martini," Pam said, closing the door behind her, putting her bag down beside Sherry on the floor. "Th' *nice* Martini."

Martini said, "Yah!"

"The Gin," Pam North said. "The Sherry."

"Yah!" said Gin. "Yah-ah!" said Sherry.

The three of them regarded her through blue eyes, Sherry with head on one side, since her eyes had never tracked. They continued to speak. Martini, who set the pace in all feline matters, was the angriest. She was very angry.

14

Pam reached out to touch the little, violent Siamese and Martini produced a "Yah!" which was at least half snarl and went off, swishing her tail.

"I'm very sorry," Pam North said, formally. "I really planned to come home last night. But the timetable was wrong because it wasn't daylight saving any longer, and this morning it was too nice. Didn't Martha feed you?"

The cats, with one voice, assured Pamela North that they had not been fed; that they were never fed; that at the residence of Mr. and Mrs. Gerald North, cats were abandoned to starvation. Pam did not believe a word of this, and told them so. Nevertheless, she went first of all to the kitchen, moving in a swarm of cats. At dinner time, three cats were twenty cats; if Siamese, twenty desperate in their crying out. They screamed up at Pam as they moved around her feet, creating, with long bodies and dark tails, patterns of infinite anxiety. Sherry reared to snag claws in the wool of fall coat, and to receive the sharpest of "No's!" for her trouble. Gin leaped to the counter to assist in the opening of cans. They fell on "junior beef," three lifted tails quivering with enthusiasm. One didn't, certainly, come home to an empty apartment.

The morning's mail was waiting; a note from Martha also was waiting, on top of the mail.

"Mr. Mutton called," Martha had written. At least, it looked like "Mutton." "Said you'd be back after dinner. Gin threw up breakfast. Out of steel wool."

It was all clear enough, except for Mr. Mutton, who was utterly unlikely. Gin had eaten too fast, as she was inclined to. Steel wool did run out. But Mr. Mutton did not telephone. Mr. Mutton did not exist. Martha's fidelity was great, her cooking excellent. But as a passer-on of such trifles as telephone messages Martha was open to improvement, although she remained beyond it. Mr. Mutton had called to say (or be told?) that Pamela North would return after dinner. Pam shook her head. She laid the note aside. Time might clarify Mr. Mutton; on the other hand, this might be the last she ever heard of him. There was precedent for either outcome.

There was no letter from Jerry. Bergdorf and Saks and Lord & Taylor were having sales. Jerry's club had something to say to Jerry. *Who's Who in America* also sought communication with him; it would be wanting him to bring his biography up to date, which he had not done for almost a month. Pam put these aside, pending his return. It occurred to Pam that even three cats did not actually fill an apartment, however they animated it. "Why," Pam asked Martini, who then returned from the kitchen, her mood improved — "why do so many authors seem to live in San Francisco?" Martini jumped to Pam's lap and settled down to distribute cat hairs. It was fortunate, Pam thought, not for the first time, that she was not particularly fond of dark clothing; it was remarkable how nearly white a Siamese cat's fur turned out to be when it had left a Siamese cat.

Pam picked up the morning papers, which were under the mail, and which she had read on the train from her week end in the country. Under the papers there was a square, stiff envelope. It bore a printed caution: "Do Not Bend." It bore a printed explanation: "Voice-Scriber Record." It was addressed, in pencil, scrawlingly, to Mr. Gerald North.

Pam turned it over in her hands, seeking a return address and finding none. She tried to decipher the postmark and failed. The envelope had not, she realized, been sent through the canceling machine, for reasons no doubt having to do with not bending. It had been postmarked by hand, and hurriedly. It might, so far as she could tell, have come from almost anywhere in the world — no, from anywhere in the United States.

She knew the machine called a Voice-Scriber; Jerry used one at his office. It was a compact recording phonograph, in essence. Into it — or half of it, the recording half — Jerry dictated.

17

From the other half of it, the transcriber, Jerry's secretary typed what Jerry had said. Now and then, Jerry brought home his half, which fitted neatly into a carrying case and weighed only about fifteen pounds, and spent an evening talking into it — while the cats, frantic to discover to whom he talked, with Pam elsewhere, yammered at his study door. One of the advantages of the Voice-Scriber was that its small records could be mailed conveniently from dictator to typist.

This one, it appeared, was for some reason retracing its steps. Well, it, too, would have to wait until Jerry — She lifted the envelope to lay it on top of the communication from *Who's Who* and stopped. Was it really *Mr.* Gerald North? Or was it *Mrs.* Gerald North? She studied the scrawl. She couldn't, she slowly realized, be certain either way. But if to her —?

It has never been said of Pamela North — at least not said by anyone who knows her — that she is sluggish of imagination. Out of the most minor of inconsistencies, Pamela North has been known to create the most unlikely of melodramas. Charged with this, she has an answer ready: It has been her experience that unlikely melodrama is the likeliest to happen of anything in the world. "Particularly," she adds, "to people who know Bill Weigand." Not even Acting Captain William Weigand, Homicide Squad, Manhattan West, New York Police Department, denies this, although sometimes speculating on the relationship in time between chicken and egg.

What now occurred to Pam North, as she turned the Voice-Scriber record over in her hands, was that something had happened to Jerry, far away and alone in San Francisco. Momentarily, she considered the possibility that he was, for reasons she might come to later, held a prisoner in Chinatown, but this she rejected. She had seen San Francisco's Chinatown and been unimpressed. New York's was smaller, to be sure, but, to Pam, beyond comparison more devious. But elsewhere, in that most gaily exciting of smaller cities, anything, she thought, might happen. Since Jerry was there, and without her, anything might happen to him.

Suppose – well, suppose something had. Suppose that (for reasons she would come to later) he was in a position where he could not communicate with her more simply, but had access to a Voice-Scriber. Suppose he had got somebody to mail this record to her. (He had not mailed it himself, or, at any rate, not addressed it.) Suppose his safety somehow depended on her hearing his recorded message.

But on the other hand, suppose that Jerry had merely wanted to talk to her, and taken this

19

way. Suppose he had been lonely on the other edge of the continent and had wished to say — well, put it, to say, "Hello, Pam. How are you, lady? How are the little cats?" Jerry did not often do such things; on the other hand, he had sometimes done them.

She looked once more at the address. The more she looked at it, the more sure she was that it read "Mrs." not "Mr." Gerald North.

"It isn't just curiosity," she told Martini. Martini said, "Yah" in a tone combining irritation and skepticism. "Well, it isn't," Pam said. "I've got to go see."

She went. The cats had never been more put out in their lives, but Pam went all the same. She carried the record in her hand, since there was no room in her bag.

She found a cab with little trouble and gave the address of Jerry's office. The cab went up Fifth, through moderate traffic, turned right in the Thirties, crossed Madison and stopped in the block beyond it. The block was a quiet one, in which some residences quietly held their own in the face of trade; in which trade was, for the most part, suitably dignified. North Books, Inc., occupied the fourth, and top, floor of a building which was as self-effacing as a building might be.

Mrs. North's cab stopped in front of the building. A station wagon which had fallen in behind it near Washington Square passed the cab but, a few doors farther along the street, pulled to the curb and stopped.

Mrs. North went into a small lobby and an elderly man, sitting at a small table, reading *Time* magazine of the week before, looked up at her. He peered through rimless glasses; then he removed them.

"Oh," he said, "hello, Mrs. North."

"Good evening, Mr. Helder," Pam said. "Isn't it a beautiful evening?"

"Won't last," Sven Helder told her. "Want to go up?" Then he sighed.

"I'm afraid I do, please," Pam North said. "I hate to bother you."

"Can't be helped," Sven Helder told her, and put *Time* magazine, open, spine up, on the table. "Probably," he added. He turned a ledger toward her. "Have to sign in," he said.

Pam North put purse and envelope on the table and signed in. She added, "North Books, Inc.," after her name. Sven Helder looked at her signature with care. He took a large watch from a pocket and looked at it. He wrote "2132" after North Books. Then he got up, pushing himself up with both hands on the little table. He led the way to one of the two elevators and led the way into it. The elevator awoke and seemed to rub its eyes; it started up, not hurrying.

"Nobody up there," Sven Helder said.

"I suppose not," Pam said.

"Nobody in the building," Sven Helder told her, as they trundled between the second floor and the third. "You're the only one." There was resigned accusation in his tone.

"I'm sorry," Pam said.

"Can't be helped," Sven Helder said. "What I'm here for, I guess." He sighed deeply.

"I won't be long," Pam said, between third and fourth.

"Doesn't make much difference, does it," Sven Helder asked her, slowly, making cautious approach. He stopped ten inches below the floor level. "Go too high she can jam," he said.

"It's perfectly all right," Pam said, and stepped up. "Ring when you want me," Helder said, and sighed, and closed the sliding door. The elevator began to inch downward.

Pam unlocked the double doors lettered "North Books, Inc." She went into the dark offices – the almost dark offices. Some light sifted in from windows; in New York it is never wholly dark. The offices, as they always did, seemed much larger at night. Pam found herself, and this again as always, wondering who sat at the many desks and what they did at them. Ideas formed in a mind, and words were found for them; the ideas were communicated, in varying degrees of accuracy, to other minds.

That was the gist of it; but between, many people sat at many desks, and at machines, also. Tall filing cases, like those near the door, were filled with — with what? Pam turned on lights. She went among the desks to Jerry's book-lined office in a corner. She turned on lights there.

She could play back from Jerry's recorder, instead of from the other thing, whatever it was, on Miss Corning's desk. That way, Pam thought, she wouldn't have to use the earphones. Earphones made her feel shut in.

She found the recorder. She took the record from its envelope and dropped the envelope, absently, in a wastepaper basket. She put the record on the turntable and set it going. There was only a faint hum, first. Then there was a voice; a woman's voice. It was faint, as if the speaker had failed to hold the microphone close enough to lips. Yet it was distinct, and for all the present smallness of the captured sound, Pam felt that the voice itself had been raised, excited.

"You must be crazy," the voice said. "Why would I —?"

"Because you have no choice," another voice said.

A man had spoken this time; spoken sharply, breaking in. His voice, also, had been raised; it had an oddly metallic texture, but that might

23

be the machine's distortion. There was a moment's pause. Then the woman laughed. The laughter seemed high to Pam North, listening; seemed too high by far.

"You'll huff and you'll puff," the voice said. "You'll blow the girl down."

"More," the man said. "Much more, if necessary."

"Really," the woman said. "You've lost your mind, haven't you? Megalomania, isn't it? To save your withered little ego you want me — My God!"

"We're not going over that again," the man said, rhyming the word with "rain." "If you need the money, I'll make good what you'd lose."

"Everything else aside, how would you know?" the woman asked. "How would anybody? And what's that got to do with it? I've spent a year on it. More than a year. Count all the time it was happening. All the time you —"

"We've been over that," the man's voice said, cutting in again, now harsh. "You made yourself clear. You're very good at that sort of thing."

"Clarity," she said. "The fine edge of clarity, remember? Too fine an edge, I gather. Too —"

"I want the copies," the man said. "Damn you, if you think —"

24

"See my agent," the woman said, and laughed again.

He said, "Don't laugh!" He must have spoken very loudly. "I tell you, quit laughing!"

"The withered little ego!" the woman said. "The poor, trembling little man! When I re-member —"

"Don't," the man said. "I tell you — *don't!*"

"Pompous little man," the woman said, and now her voice, also, was further raised — or she had moved nearer the microphone. "Frightened little man. Your reputation. Your precious little job. Oh, they'll laugh, all right. Don't think they won't laugh. They'll say, 'You know who he is, don't you? He's the one who doesn't come up smiling. He's the prating, sniveling little man who couldn't —' "

"That was a lie," the man said. He called her a name. His voice was high, violent.

"Suppose it was?" she said. "Literally, a lie. Essentially, the truth. Call it a symbol. You talked about symbols, remember? I didn't for-get." She laughed again.

Then there was a moment of silence before the man spoke once more. His voice now had a strange timbre; there was a curious detachment in his voice; it was almost, Pam thought, as if he spoke to ears which could no longer hear him speak.

"I told you not to laugh," the man said.

25

"Remember, I told you that. I gave you a chance, remember. I —"

The man's voice was harsh, monotonous. It did not, in tone, threaten. But the woman screamed.

It was a tiny, faraway scream, as it came from the record — a thin scream; it was as if a doll had screamed.

"It will be like killing a snake," the man said, in the same harsh, uninflected voice. "A small, bright, deadly snake."

"You ca —" the woman's voice said, and then there was a harsh, guttural sound — a sound made uglily of effort and of pain; perhaps of terror. There was no other sound for a minute or more. Then there was a sharp sound as if something of metal, or perhaps of glass, had fallen against a surface equally hard.

After that, there was only the low humming of the machine, as the record turned slowly on its table. No other sound came from the record.

Pamela North stood and watched the record turn; stood and waited for the voices to resume; stood and after a moment began to tremble a little, thinking that she had heard murder. She stopped the little machine, then. She took the record from it, and held the record in both hands and looked at it. It was only a little record. From a record like that one might hear a song.

26

It was while she stood so, holding the record, that Pam heard a sound from the outer office. It was a small sound; it was as if someone, moving carefully, had touched the back of a chair, and moved it against another chair, or against a desk. Pam turned toward the door she had left open behind her.

As she turned, the lights went off in the outer office.

Pam was quick, then. She was quick to the light switch by the door. After she had flicked it down she stood motionless, in semi-darkness, wishing it a deeper darkness. She listened, and heard no further sound. She tried to make her breathing soundless.

When still there was no repeated sound from the outer office, and in its shadows no movement, Pam thought that she might have been wrong. There had been someone there, of course. Someone had put out the lights. But could that have been Sven Helder, not — not the man whose voice had talked of killing? Perhaps he had come to get her, seen the lights on and not seen her, turned off the lights to go grumbling down again. Perhaps —

She should, she realized, have remembered the telephone sooner. She lifted it, now, and started to dial a familiar number before she realized there was no tone.

As she realized this, she realized, too, that

there would not be. There would be a light on the switchboard in the receptionist's cubbyhole by the door. There would be nothing else. If she was to use the telephone, she must reach the switchboard. But to reach it, she must cross the outer office. If she got that far, she would have a chance to run for it.

She waited for several more minutes, as motionless, as quiet, as she could wait — as acutely listening. There was no sound from the outer office. She thought of the washroom off Jerry's office as a hiding place; at once rejected it as a trap. She must get out.

She moved, then. Her shoes were quickly removed, held in her hands. On stockinged feet she went softly through the door from Jerry's office and then, instead of crossing the outer office directly, along the wall to her right. She would move a few feet and then stop, to listen. And now, somewhere — it seemed everywhere — she could hear the breathing of another person.

She had been standing by Miss Corning's desk, her hands resting lightly on it. Then she crouched a little, made herself small, strained eyes and ears, moved in little steps toward safety. She moved among other desks, around them, feeling each desk as somehow a barrier to pursuit. She moved with each step nearer the door, and safety.

She was almost at the door, could almost

reach it, when she heard footsteps behind her. He had been waiting — and she knew it now too late — in the concealment of high, metal filing cases. She tried to turn.

She was not quick enough.

Sven Helder turned his copy of *Time* magazine up-side-down on the table in front of him, extracted his large watch from a pocket, and looked at the watch. As he had known it would, the watch showed the hour to be ten-thirty. Mr. Helder picked up *Time* magazine, closed it, and put it in the drawer of the table. He looked at the ledger in front of him and re-informed himself that Mrs. Gerald North had gone up at 2132 — Helder was a retired chief petty officer, and liked a log kept in a ship-shape manner — and had not come down. Helder sighed deeply and shook his head heavily. It was like them.

She knew, she had been there often enough to know, that the building closed at ten-thirty. The front doors were locked, then. Helder made his final rounds then. After them he had his sandwiches and coffee; after that he went to sleep in his room in the basement. These things happened nightly, except on Sunday. Mrs. Gerald North knew that as well as anyone. It was merely that she was, after all, like the rest of them. She had no regard for regulations.

Helder got up heavily and went to the elevator. He clanged the door closed and started it up; at the fourth floor, he clanged the door open. If she hadn't heard the elevator by now, she wouldn't hear anything. Nevertheless, he yelled, "Hey, Mrs. North!" Nobody answered.

Helder made a remark under his breath, ran the elevator to floor level — *he* wasn't going to step up — and went to the closed doors of North Books, Inc. There was no light showing through the glass panels. Nevertheless, he pushed at the doors and found them unlocked. He poked his head into the dark offices, and again called Pamela North. But by then he knew what had happened.

She had gone down the stairs, instead of ringing for him. She must have gone — let's see now. She must have gone when, about ten, he'd gone down to the head for a minute. Anyway, she clearly wasn't there now.

He closed the door to North Books, Inc., and locked it, as Mrs. North had neglected to do. He went back to the elevator and trundled it down. He supposed she had meant all right; probably she'd meant to save him a trip. She was like that. But she ought to have remembered that he'd have to check up on her unless she signed herself out. Well — there you were. Even the best of them.

He looked at his log when he was back at the table. He knew he had not made a mistake, and

30

he hadn't. Mrs. North had not signed herself out. He shook his head over this. He would have thought better of her. He went to the double doors of the building. He stepped out of them and stood just outside for a moment. It was a pleasant night, warm for late October. Not that the weather was to be trusted, in the fall. It could snow any day, now.

He watched a station wagon pull away from the curb two doors down the street. He looked east and west along the street, and saw no one. He went back inside and locked the doors behind him. He started on his last round of the night.

III

Tuesday, October 28: 10 A.M. to 2:25 P.M.

Acting Captain William Weigand sat in his small office, at his rather battered desk, in the West Twentieth Street station house, and dealt with routine. There was not, and had not been for several months, much that was not routine. People continued to kill other people, of course. They killed with guns. In certain areas they killed with knives. They killed with blackjacks, and with the leather of shoes and sometimes with their fists. They left bodies on the streets, and in the parks and in the North and East rivers. By and large, they were caught, or would be caught. By and large, they were taken care of on the precinct level.

The takings off were, nevertheless, part of the routine of Homicide, West. Reports came in; reports were read, initialed, passed along. Reports passed over Weigand's desk, found their way to the desk of Deputy Chief Inspector Artemus O'Malley; went on from there, through channels, to files. Excitement was no part of it; imagination did not enter in. Finger-prints and laundry marks, known associates, known methods, known feuds, most of all informers — these things entered in, made up the routine. These things made it hard to get away with murder.

It had been a light night. There had been a knifing in Harlem, solved already. There had been a brawl in a Village bar and it had ended in homicide — homicide not intended, hardly realized. And the Hudson had given up a body.

The last alone awaited solution. The body had not yet been identified. It was that of a small man in his thirties — five-feet-six, one hundred thirty-five, brown hair and eyes, scar (probably old gunshot wound) upper right chest; no recent dental work, and a good deal needed; brown suit from a Broadway clothier, no cleaner's marks; blue shirt, cuffs frayed, laundry mark being checked; brown shoes, recently half-soled; blue socks. No hat found with body. Fingerprints being checked.

Bill Weigand initialed, consigned to an out basket. Sergeant Aloysius Mullins came in and said, "Morning, Loot, I mean Captain. Got an identification on the North River one."

"Right," Bill said, and reached for the report. Mullins gave it to him, and crossed the room to his own desk.

The small man with the gunshot scar had

been Harry Eaton, burglar by occupation and no master of his trade. He had been thirty-two years old. He had spent seven years of the last ten in jail, and had been on parole when he died. He had been three times convicted of felonies; another conviction would have meant life imprisonment. That, at any rate, no longer hung over the bruised head of little Harry Eaton. He had died of strangulation, having first been knocked unconscious by a blow behind the right ear. He had been throttled. And that was uncharacteristic. Reading it, Bill Weigand said, "Hm-m."

"Yeah," Mullins said, from his desk. "You've got to where somebody used his hands."

Bill nodded. They did not need to discuss the minor oddity of that. Men like Eaton were never good life risks; they fell into bad company. They rather often got themselves killed — they went out of their rackets, they held out on a split, they threatened to pass on information. For such misdemeanors they were often beaten, sometimes fatally. They were sometimes shot. But it did not often happen that someone put hands on their throats, and squeezed life out of them. This is an awkward way of murder; a blackjack is handier and, unless circumstances make so noisy a method undesirable, a gun is handier still. Strangulation — except, of course, in the case of "muggers," where murder is incidental — is a method of amateurs, and violent ones at that.

However, it was not much to go on. Eaton remained routine. Bill took the first report out of the basket, clipped the identification report to it, and put both back in.

"He lived down on Sullivan Street," Mullins said. "Two-room, cold water, fifth floor. The precinct boys have been around."

Bill Weigand waited. There was more coming.

"Coupla funny things," Mullins said. "One, he'd stolen a dictating machine somewhere. Thing you dictate into. Funny thing to steal."

Nothing, Bill reminded him, was a funny thing to steal; not for a man like Eaton. Men like Eaton picked up what they could find, and disposed of it where they could. But Mullins did not need to be told this, and Bill Weigand continued to wait.

"Well," Mullins said, "seems like Eaton had written a book. About how he'd been a burglar."

"My God!" Bill said.

"Yeah," Mullins said. "Like that. Seems he sent it to two-three publishers and they all turned it down."

"Go on," Weigand said.

"Yeah," Mullins said. "That's right. Mr. North was one of them. There was a letter from him in Eaton's place."

Bill Weigand said, "Oh."

"So there we are," Mullins said. "I thought I'd better tell you."

Bill Weigand nodded. He said, "Right." He stood up.

"Well," he said, "what are we waiting for, Sergeant?"

Mullins couldn't think of anything.

Three cats yammered at Martha. They sat and yammered; they clawed at her skirt and yammered; they reared themselves against kitchen counters and spoke their anger and chagrin in the harsh accents of cats with blue eyes and masked faces. They spoke of neglect, of the collapse of the routine by which a cat prefers to live; they spoke of hunger. Most of all, they spoke of hunger.

"What's the matter with you cats?" Martha asked them, hanging her coat in the kitchen closet. "What's all the fussin'?"

Spoken to, the three cats raised their voices in answer. Martini went to an empty tin pie plate and put her foot on it; Gin leaped to the counter which contained small cans of prepared beef, for juniors, and pointed at the cans. Sherry sang a dirge, in a voice pitched higher than the other voices.

"Now that's funny," Martha told the cats.

"You know you've had your breakfast. You're trying to put one over."

They weren't, the cats said. Had breakfast indeed! They had never eaten.

"Well," Martha said, and stood in the middle of the kitchen and looked around. "It is funny."

Their food pan was empty. That could be explained. They had eaten their breakfast and forgotten it. But their water bowl also was empty, and they would not have drunk a bowl of water since breakfast. And Mrs. North would not have forgotten; Mrs. North now and then forgot things — to order steel wool, for example. But she did not forget cats.

Martha said "hm-m-m" and went in search. The search did not take long. Mrs. North was not in the apartment. And — she had been. She had got home from the country.

Her week-end case, still packed, stood on the bedroom floor. But neither bed had been occupied. Martha said "hm-m-m" again and then, to the cats who followed her, "All right, come on." She fed the cats. They ate with fervor. Martha watched them; she had been wrong to think they had been trying to put one over. They had been hungry cats. Martini stopped midway, hurried to the water bowl, lapped anxiously, hurried back, found her place again at the tin pie pan. Thirsty cats, too. Hm-m-m.

Martha went back into the living room. Yes,

Mrs. North had come home all right. She had opened mail, and put aside mail addressed to Mr. North. It was a funny thing. Mrs. North had come home, she had fed the cats — Martha had washed the used food pan before she left the afternoon before; it had been filled and put down again. Mrs. North had opened mail. She had — yes, she had smoked a cigarette. Then she had gone out and not come back.

It is perhaps to Mrs. North's credit that Martha assumed only disaster. Mrs. North was not a fly-by-night; if she had flown and not returned, and not made provision for the cats, only disaster could explain. Other attractive women might, with husbands distant, flutter prettily from the nest; Martha had heard of such, and known a few. But Mrs. North would not. (Or, if she did, she would be home in time to feed her cats.)

There was that policeman friend of theirs; he would know what to do. She looked in the Norths' address book and found a number and dialed it. She heard, "Homicide, Sergeant Stein" and asked for Acting Captain Weigand. He had just gone out. "No," Martha said, "I guess not," when she was asked if anyone else could help. Going to a policeman who was a friend was one thing; going to the police another. But she had to go to somebody.

She telephoned North Books, Inc., and

talked to Mr. North's secretary. Mr. North was in San Francisco, at the St. Francis. Martha got pencil and paper; she began to compose a telegram.

Gerald North, sitting by the window of his room at the St. Francis, poured himself another cup of coffee. He looked down on Union Square, on which the morning sun was shining. He watched cars turning into, nosing out of, the parking lot under the square and thought that New York might copy. He was unhurried and at peace, and he had only a slight headache. It had been a lengthy night, but worth it, and fun too. He had the manuscript he had come after, and the promise of another. He had an unforgettable memory of the harbor and the bridge, as the sun sank, seen through the great window of a little house which clung to a hillside. He had a double bedroom reservation on the City of San Francisco, eastward bound, and another on the Commodore Vanderbilt from Chicago. The evening before he had got a letter from Pam, and she was fine (but not too fine) and starting off for a week end in the country with the Thompsons. Jerry North lighted a second cigarette, and somebody knocked at the door. He said, "Come in," to what would be the waiter after the breakfast things.

But a bellboy came in and said, "Telegram, Mr. North," and brought the familiar envelope across the room. Jerry signed and left money on the tray; he opened the telegram as the boy closed the door behind him. He read:

"Mrs. North come home last night went away again somewhere and not back this morning to feed cats stop no message either stop worried because not way she is stop thought you ought to know stop best wishes – Martha."

Contentment vanished as he read. He knew Martha; also he knew Pamela. Like Martha, he envisioned only disaster. Pam had got herself into something again. He reread the telegram. Feeding the cats – that was the crux of it. Otherwise, one might envision a sick friend or importunate relative, of whom Pam had one or two. But Pam's conviction that cats should be fed on schedule was equaled only by that of the cats themselves.

"Damn!" Jerry said to himself. "Oh – damn!" He stubbed out his cigarette. But, sitting on the bed, reaching for the telephone, he lighted another. He got the porter's desk. It was an emergency. The porter's desk would do what it could and call him back.

He waited, looking across the room, through the window, seeing nothing of what he saw. He jabbed out the new cigarette; almost at once he lighted another. He tried to reason with his feeling; tried to tell himself that there were a dozen explanations – and thought of half a dozen. He did not believe any of them.

He called himself an emotional fool. He said, and now he spoke aloud, "Damn it. Why don't you ever wait? Why don't you –?" He spoke across a continent to Pamela North. The telephone rang and he snatched at it. The porter's desk had managed a reservation on a TWA plane leaving in a little less than an hour. It was, Jerry told them, hearing the tightness in his own voice, good of them. Would they arrange to cancel his reservation on the streamliner? They would send up for the tickets.

Jerry called off a luncheon date. He packed. He found that he was picking things up before he had a hold on them; he found the lock on his suitcase resistant to too hurried fingers. He was being a fool; he was being all kinds of a fool. Of course, Pam would be all right. She was always all right. She –

"Damn!" Jerry said, and yanked at the strap of his suitcase. *Be careful, Pam. Be careful!*

There was no real connection. The little man who had lived in these two bare rooms, chilly and dark even on a day so bright and warm for late October, had decided he was a writer. He

41

could write a book about what had happened to him. Actually, he had written it; one could say that, if one felt generous. He had a manuscript to prove it, or had had. Bill Weigand had it now, and read a few pages. The poor guy, Bill thought, and put the manuscript down. It would have to be read, he supposed; conceivably, there might be something useful somewhere in it. It would, however, be a job for — He looked at Mullins thoughtfully. Well, then, for Sergeant Stein. But there was no real connection.

The little, inept burglar named Harry Eaton had sent his book to publishers, having somehow discovered that that is what one does with books. He had sent it to four publishers, North Books, Inc., among them. North Books, Inc., had sent regrets, polite but brief, on — Bill looked at the letter again — August 18. The letter was signed "Gerald North, per E.C." Jerry had written a memo "Tell him no" and clipped it to the manuscript. Bill could see him doing it. It was no connection at all. There was no conceivable reason why Bill Weigand, Acting Captain, Homicide, Manhattan West, should feel the beginning of that nagging sense of urgency, that need to run to keep up, he so inevitably felt on cases with which the Norths were involved.

There was not much else in the room. Another suit; two shirts and three pairs of underwear shorts in a drawer, a stained tie hanging over a nail on the inside of the closet door. They were printing the place, as a matter of routine. They would, as a matter of routine, check serial numbers on the Voice-Scriber – the only shining object in the dusty rooms – and so, in time, determine the owner. It was as routine as it had seemed. Routine would solve it. Routine was automatic; it would be followed without direction.

"Suppose you get on to the people who make these things," Bill Weigand said to Mullins, indicating the Voice-Scriber. "Get a line on who owns it."

"Me?" Mullins said. "You want I should?"

It was not really a job for Mullins. It was a job for the precinct; it hardly rated a detective, first grade, let alone a sergeant.

"O.K., Loot," Mullins said. "I mean Captain. I guess you're right. It'll be a screwy one."

He hadn't, Weigand pointed out, said that. "As good as," Mullins told him. Weigand thought a moment; then he said, "Right. Perhaps I did. Hurry it up?"

"O.K., Loot," Mullins said. "I mean –"

"I know what you mean," Weigand said. "Get going, Sergeant."

Mullins got going. So, leaving routine in experienced hands, did Weigand. He went to a

43

telephone; he called North Books, Inc. He found that Mr. North was still in San Francisco. He was expected back Friday morning. Was there anything Miss Corning could do to help the Captain?

A man named Eaton, who had written a book called – called *what?* "My Life in Crime?" She didn't remember any Eaton.

There had been a letter, Bill told her. The letter rejected Mr. Eaton's life in crime. She had signed Mr. North's name, initialed under it.

But that she did all the time. No doubt she had this time. She would look it up in the files. In August? August 18? She would look it up.

"I wish you would," Bill told her. "Not that it means anything in particular, so far as I know. What I'd really like to know, did Mr. North have any personal contact with Eaton, do you know?"

So far as Miss Corning knew, he had had none. But she was uncertain about it. She did not remember that Eaton had come personally to the office, but she was not sure he had not. She did not, in short, remember anything whatever about Harry Eaton. This was reasonable. Bill Weigand said, "Right."

He had work to do, Bill Weigand told himself. He was a policeman, on the city payroll. Routine was reaching his battered desk in the West Twentieth Street station house and stopping there, dammed up by his absence. A petty burglar was strangled instead of shot; it developed that he once had had his reminiscences rejected by, among others, North Books, Inc. In a day when every candlestick maker had a book in him and most let it out, this was not surprising.

Already, Bill Weigand told himself, sternly, he had wasted a morning on a case for the precinct, merely because the name of North had occurred in it. Now he would —

But there was no great harm, Bill decided, in wasting another ten minutes or so, merely to allay that nagging sense of urgency. He dialed another telephone number, this one familiar. If Jerry North had had any contact with little Harry Eaton, any contact of even remote interest, he would have mentioned it to Pam. The Norths mentioned all things to each other. Jerry would not dream of concealing a small burglar, or a book titled: "My Life in Crime."

The telephone signaled that it was ringing in the North apartment. Then it was answered.

"Hello, Martha," Bill said. "This is Weigand. Is Mrs. North — ?"

"She's gone," Martha said. "That's what it is. Something's happened to her. You can't tell me."

"Listen," Bill Weigand said. "What? Who's gone?"

"I tried to get you," Martha said. "You weren't there. So I wired Mr. North. He's in San Francisco."

"Please, Martha," Bill Weigand said. "You mean Mrs. North isn't there? You don't know where she is?"

Martha told him, then. She told him all of it, with special reference to the hunger of the cats. "You better come right here and do something," Martha ended.

No doubt there were a dozen explanations. The absence of Pam North from her apartment at one-thirty of a Tuesday afternoon did not spell disaster.

"Right," Bill Weigand said. "I'll be over."

He drove downtown. He did not drive like a policeman in a hurry, but he did not loiter. Martha let him in. She told the story again. She had it ready, now. She had finished cleaning the apartment in mid-afternoon of the day before. She had gone home to Harlem. Mrs. North had already telephoned that she would not be home to dinner. Mrs. North had come home during the evening. She had fed the cats. She had opened letters from Bergdorf and Saks and Lord & Taylor. The captain could see the envelopes and the enclosures. She had put her week-end bag in the bedroom, leaving it packed.

46

Then she had gone somewhere. She had been gone all night. And — she had not returned in the morning to feed the cats.

"Maybe she went to spend the night with a friend," Bill Weigand said.

"The cats," Martha said.

"Perhaps something's happened to Mr. North and she's flown west," Bill said.

"Even then, she wouldn't forget the cats," Martha told him. "You know that, Captain. What you pretend for?"

He did not know why he pretended. He went through the apartment and found nothing Martha had not found. He went through Pam North's desk, and found only what one might expect to find. (This included two rather lengthy columns of figures, added to totals which failed by a considerable margin to coincide. Idly, Bill Weigand added one of the columns. Pam had been wrong. He resisted the temptation to add the other column. Pam had been, he supposed, balancing a checkbook or working on a budget.)

There was nothing. She had come home, fed cats, smoked a cigarette, looked at the mail and then —

It was, at a guess, something in the mail. He called Martha back from the kitchen. She had, he assumed, brought the mail up that day. Or had Mrs. North brought it up herself?

47

Martha had brought it up, with the morning papers.

"Try to remember," Bill said. "The papers. These letters for Mr. North. The three she opened. Was that all the mail?"

"Don't seem like I remember —" Martha began, and then broke off. "Seems like I do," she said. "There was something else. Bigger."

"A package?" Weigand asked. "A bigger envelope?"

"Seems like it was another letter," Martha said. "Jus' not the same shape."

She had not paid much attention. She tried now to remember. Another envelope, almost certainly. She thought it had been square. She hadn't put her mind to it.

She could not come closer, however she tried. But perhaps, Bill thought, it was something. There had been a squarish envelope in the mail; Mrs. North had taken it with her when she went. But where one went from there he didn't, at the moment, know.

He called headquarters and got the Missing Persons Bureau. He said, "Look, Joe, this could be important." He gave a description of Pamela North, speaking rapidly. With Martha's aid, he described what she probably had been wearing — a beige woolen dress with brown cuffs; a suède coat, no hat on her bright hair. He was asked to hold it, and did. It took a few minutes.

48

Then Joe said, "Nope, sorry. No report."

"You'll get it out?" Bill asked, and was promised that it would go out with expedition. He hung up, then dialed his own office.

There were two things. One was a telegram from Gerald North. "Martha says Pam missing. Flying back. Will you do what you can?" The other was Sergeant Mullins, in person, reporting progress.

They had been lucky, for once. A Voice-Scriber with the serial number as given had been sold directly by the regional sales office of the company and not, as might have happened, by an agency anywhere in the east — or in the country, for that matter. This had made the check easy.

The machine had been sold to a Miss Hilda Godwin, of 2 Elm Lane, Manhattan.

"It's in the Village, somewhere," Mullins said. "Want I should drop around? If I can find it?"

"I'll meet you there," Bill said. He told Mullins where he was, and why.

"Jeeze," Mullins said. "Like I said. A screwy one."

Bill did not argue it. He did what he could to reassure Martha, which was little. She was to get in touch with his office at once if anything turned up — preferably, Mrs. North. He said a brief goodbye to Sherry, who would permit it,

49

and to Gin, who remained across the room. Martini had disappeared as completely as her mistress. Bill Weigand walked from the Norths' apartment to Sixth Avenue and Eighth Street, where he consulted a traffic patrolman as to the probable location of Elm Lane. He walked through Christopher Street to Seventh Avenue, where he consulted another traffic patrolman. He walked part way back through Christopher Street, turned left, turned left again, and was back on Seventh Avenue, this time at Greenwich. He consulted another traffic patrolman there and went west into a labyrinth, and came on Elm Lane just when he had abandoned hope. It was a short street, and no elms grew on it. No. 2 was on a corner. Acting Captain Weigand stopped in front of it and looked at it in astonishment.

He knew New York, which is various, particularly below Fourteenth Street. But he could not remember he had ever seen a house quite like this little house.

Its smallness was the chief thing. It was, he thought, the smallest house he had ever seen and been inclined to call a house. In width, it could hardly be more than fifteen feet; there seemed scarcely space for the flight of stairs up to the doorway, for the polished brass rails on either side of the stairs. Yet there was space for the door, and for two narrow windows, leaded, holding glass fabricated in another day. There was a brass knocker on the white door.

Along the intersecting street – Brock Street – the little house ran for perhaps forty feet. The lot ran deeper by some distance; a wooden fence shielded what was no doubt a garden. Midway of the fence, there were double doors.

The little house was two stories high. It had, of all things, a mansard roof. It was proud and dainty amid taller, square buildings, most of them the conventional brick dwellings of older New York; all of them neatly flattened after the appropriate four floors; all of them, obviously, divided now into apartments. All but the little house. There was not, surely, enough of it to divide.

Bill Weigand went up the flight of white steps to the white door, feeling that he should first have wiped his feet. He pressed a button and heard a bell ring. Then he waited. He rang again, and as he did so a prowl car came up to the curb, making little of itself, and Mullins got out. He looked at the house and said that he would be damned. He joined Bill at the door. Bill rang again and waited again. Nobody came to the white door.

"Nobody home," Mullins said, after several more minutes.

Weigand agreed with him.

It stopped them, of course. It was one of

those things, and one which happens as frequently to policemen as to others. You call on someone unexpectedly, and the someone is not at home. There is nothing further to do, no matter how a sense of the need for haste nags at your mind. You cannot break down a sedate white door, policeman or not. You can merely go away and try again later.

Acting Captain William Weigand and Sergeant Aloysius Mullins walked down the white stairway, which would just accommodate the two of them abreast. At the foot of it, a tall man waited them politely. When they had reached the sidewalk, he went up the stairs. He rang the bell. Weigand and Mullins regarded him. They waited. He rang the bell several times.

"I'm afraid," Weigand said, "that Miss Godwin is not at home."

The tall man turned and looked down at Weigand and Sergeant Mullins. He was a handsome man in, perhaps, his middle forties. His features were regular, his chin firm; his skin had the freshness of the massaged. He wore a dark gray suit which fitted well across square shoulders; he carried a darker gray topcoat folded neatly over his left arm. He raised his eyebrows momentarily at the two below him. Then he smiled.

"An elusive young lady," he said. "I gather you have already tried?"

"Right," Weigand told him.

The tall man looked at the police car and back at Weigand and Mullins. He raised his eyebrows again, slightly. "The police?" he said. "Surely – ?"

"Miss Godwin seems to have been robbed," Weigand told him. "Burglarized, rather. By a sneak thief. We hope she'll be able to identify some of her property."

The tall man came down the steps, shaking his head. He wore a homburg on his head. It became him. Seen closer, below the homburg, his hair was graying becomingly at the temples. He was very sorry to hear that Miss Godwin had been victimized.

"You wouldn't happen to know when Miss Godwin will be home?" Bill asked him.

He smiled and shook his head; he shrugged.

"Not our Hilda," he said. "One never does, really. She's unpredictable, of course. She may have packed up and gone anywhere. She often does, you know."

Bill Weigand shook his head, indicating that he didn't.

"But," the tall man said, "you know who she is, surely?"

The name had meant nothing; it appeared it should have. So prompted, Bill began vaguely to remember. Hilda Godwin. Hilda Godwin.

"The writer," the tall man said. "Perhaps we

are inclined to over-estimate her fame. But still —" He waited. Making, Weigand thought, almost too evident an allowance for a policeman, he waited.

"I do remember," Bill said. "The poet. They compared her to Millay — almost compared her to Millay. Several years ago, wasn't it?"

"About five," the man said. "When she was twenty. Mrs. Parker also was mentioned, by way of comparison. I believe there was even, in some quarters, passing reference to Keats." He smiled, the smile of maturity. "She has the further advantage of being beautiful," he said. "It is always desirable for a poet to have beauty."

He spoke well; it was evident he enjoyed it. His speech went well with the little house; it was less appropriate to the situation. Bill Weigand nodded, to indicate that he had heard.

"Have to try again," he said. "If you should find her, Mr. — ?"

"Wilson," the tall man said. "Bernard Wilson."

There was, it seemed to Bill Weigand, the faintest of implied suggestion that that name, also, might prove familiar. It did not.

"Wilson," Bill said, finishing his sentence. "Will you ask her to get in touch with me? Acting Captain Weigand?" He paused, momentarily, realizing that even to the uninitiated the identification he had been about to add might

54

seem strange. "Tenth precinct," he said. "The West Twentieth Street station house. She'll find it listed."

"Certainly," Mr. Wilson said. "Although — she may be anywhere by now, as I said. California, Florida. The south of France." He shook his head. "And I had stopped by to ask if I could give her tea," he added. "Unpredictable, our Hilda."

It was far from a stolen dictating machine. "Well," Bill said, "thanks."

He led the way to the police car; Mullins went around it to get behind the wheel. When Bill was in the car, Mr. Wilson crossed the sidewalk and spoke.

"By the way," he said. "What was the nature of the property you recovered? In case I should happen to find Hilda? She may merely be out to lunch, of course."

"A Voice-Scriber," Weigand said. "It's a —"

"I know," Mr. Wilson said. He shook his head. "How young writers change," he said. "I can remember —"

"Well, thanks," Bill said again. Mullins started the car. They left Mr. Bernard Wilson on the sidewalk, with whatever it was he remembered.

IV

After the first blow, she had not been hurt.
Since she had been here, she had not been
touched. She had only been locked in darkness.
She had only, at intervals, faced the blinding
light and heard the whisper behind her.

"Where?" the whisper had said; had said over
and over. "Where is it? When you tell me, I'll
let you go."

It had always been the whisper, never the
full voice. It had to be the same, or it had no
meaning. Yet she could not prove it the
same. A voice is recognized by its timbre
and by its pitch; by gradations and phrasing.
A whisper has no timbre; it may be pitched
almost at will. A whisper has no body.

The one who whispered, who had to be the
same man, was as disembodied as the
sound. The light shone in her eyes in the black
cubicle in which she was locked; the man who
held the light was invisible behind it. Now the
whisper seemed to come from the lips of a tall
man; now from those of someone much shorter.

56

But the light itself was held now high, now low. It might be that, to confuse her, the man, if he was tall, sometimes crouched; if short, sometimes stood on tiptoe. Perhaps, although she did not believe this, it was not always the same man.

It was time for him to come again, Pam thought. It must be time. Even that was better than this darkness . . .

She had wakened to the darkness, how long ago she could hardly guess. She had wakened, pain in her head, and had at first not known herself awake. Then she had thought herself blind, and had screamed. The light came on then for the first time. He had been waiting.

"Who are you?" the whisper behind the light said first. "Are you Mrs. North?"

"Yes," she said. "Oh — yes! What's happened?"

"You were sent a record," the whisper said. "You took it to your husband's office. To play it, of course. You remember that?"

She had not. But then she did.

"You killed her," Pam said. "You — wait — you called her a snake. Then you killed her."

"Who?" the whisper said. "You don't know, do you? You can't prove anything, can you?"

"I heard your voice," Pam said. "Heard — the things you said. I'll know the voice."

"Don't boast," the whisper said. "I wouldn't

57

boast. But — suppose you did? Without the record, suppose you did? There isn't anything else. Not now."

"I —" Pam began, and then stopped. "You're right, of course. Why have you done this, then?"

"I didn't find the record," the whispering man said. "The envelope, but not the record. The watchman came up too soon. Tell me where it is. When I get it, I'll let you go."

Pam did not answer. It was a lie. She did not need to be told it was a lie.

"Where is it?" the whisper repeated.

"If you find it, you'll kill me," Pam North said. "Why wouldn't you? As you did — who-ever it was."

"It's in your husband's office," the whisper said. "You hid it there. Your husband won't be back until Friday. Nobody'll find it until then. I won't kill you if you tell me where it is."

She said, "No," to that. Then the light went out. Then the door closed as she jumped toward it; held against her. Then she heard a padlock snap.

That was the first time. Since then she had not jumped at the door. Held under the unflinching light, outlined in it, her least movement, the least tensing of her muscles, was as revealing to the man who held the light as words would have been if she had said, "I'm going to jump for the door, now."

She was locked in a square room, the walls of rough boards. The room was about ten feet by ten, she could not tell how high it was. She could not reach a ceiling; jumping, she could not touch a ceiling. It was only after hours that she guessed what the room was. It was only after the night was gone that, looking up, she saw, far above, a curved line of light.

At first, this was meaningless. There was too little light to lessen the darkness; there was only this thin line, telling of light elsewhere; this part of a circle of light. The circle, she thought, would be perhaps three feet in diameter. About the diameter of —

But she could not think, at first. The pain still filled her head; the darkness was like a pressure on her body. Her mind would not work. She made it work. About three feet in diameter — a circle of three feet, more or less. An opening of that dimension, not quite closed, leading upward to light. Pam North shook her paining head. It was as if she were seeing, from below, one of the manhole covers one sees in city streets; one of the covers which, removed, let men down into a labyrinth of water mains and conduits and great sewers. But she was not —

She realized, then. She was in the coal bin of some building. The light above came around half the circumference of the badly fitting cover of the opening through which the bin was filled. Beyond the heavy board walls of the prison was the basement of the building, whatever it was, wherever it was.

The bin was empty of coal but, now realizing where she was, Pam felt the grittiness of coal under her feet. She stooped down and felt the floor, and felt the harshness of the coal dust. Unconsciously, she wiped her hand on the wool of her dress, and then, still instinctively, brushed at the fabric before she realized that she had been lying on the coal-blackened floor for an undeterminable time before she regained consciousness. I've ruined my dress, Pam North thought, inconsequentially; it was such a pretty dress . . .

It had been about two hours — she could not see her watch and so could only guess — after he came first that he came again. She heard him walking through the basement, and by the cadence of the footsteps knew it was a man. She heard his key in the padlock and faced the sound, tensing, and then the light was on her. The whisper came again.

"Well?"

Pam shook her head.

"Where is it?" the whisper said. "You'll tell me in the end, you know. I don't want to hurt you, but I can."

She had known that. She had waited for him to say that. He was right, of course. He could hurt her until she told him what he wanted to know. But, until then —

Pam shook her head again.

"You're stubborn," he whispered. "It won't do you any good. There's no need to be a fool."

"No," Pam said.

"Aren't you thirsty?" the whisperer asked. "I'd think you'd be thirsty."

She was. She nodded.

"Well?" he said.

She shook her head.

He stepped back then, the light receding, holding her until the last moment. Then the door slammed shut and the lock clicked, and there was only the darkness — only the darkness and the thin, semi-circular edge of light above.

She had been conscious of growing thirst before, but not sharply conscious. Now the idea of water began to grow in her mind; now her mouth grew dry as if dry, hot air were being forced into it. Partly, she realized, this was due to suggestion — he had spoken of thirst and her mind, even her body, responded. She could go for hours yet before thirst was more than an inconvenience, several hours before hunger was added to thirst. So that was what he planned. Hunger and thirst — and darkness. Now the darkness was the worst. It wouldn't always be.

Somebody would come. Somebody always came. *Jerry*, Pam thought, *I'm here!* But where was here?

She thought, already they'll be looking for me. Martha will come and find I'm not there; she'll know because the cats won't be fed. And then Jerry'll — But no, Jerry's in San Francisco, not here. He won't even know, and Martha'll just think I've gone some place for the night. But won't she know I'd make some arrangement about the cats? Or that I'd leave her a note? Then won't she — ?

She'll get hold of Bill, Pam thought. She knows Bill. And then he'll start looking and —

But what good will it do? What will he have to go on? He'll find out I went to the office and Mr. Helder will remember taking me up. But Mr. Helder didn't see the man who hit me, or I wouldn't be here. He must have carried me down the stairs and through the lobby when Mr. Helder was somewhere else and then to a car, of course. Then he must be strong. Then —

It went round and round in her mind. It went faster and faster, until her own thoughts seemed to dizzy her and she sat down on the gritty floor and hugged her knees in her arms and then put her head on her knees and sat so, huddled, feeling that her mind had been running. And the dryness in her throat grew, and the dryness of her lips grew.

It was longer before he came a third time. This time she merely sat as she was, huddled on the floor, and shook her head to all he said; shook her head even when he said, "You must be getting very thirsty, by now." He did not remain long the third time. He whispered, "All right, I can wait," and the light went out.

When Pam looked up again, the thin edge of light was fainter. She realized that the shortened day of late October was nearing its end. This time yesterday, Pam thought, I was getting on the train in the country, or off the train. This time yesterday, I was going home. There was water on the train — cold water at the end of the car; paper cups to hold the water. But I wasn't, thirsty and I didn't drink any water. And there was water at home, all the water in the world, and ice for the water, and I wasn't thirsty and didn't drink the water. And somewhere in this house there is water in pipes, water flowing; somewhere there's a tap and if I turned it water would rush out, frothing a little from the pressure. I could hold a glass under it and water would gush into the glass and flow over the top as I cooled the glass and wash down over the hand I held the glass in and —

How long this was, she did not know.

Now she heard a sound. It was the sound of his footsteps again. He was coming back. If she said, "Yes, I'll tell you," he would give her water. Then he would go and find the record with his voice on it — did he think there was more than that? Did he think his name had been used? Why didn't he ask? Because she would lie, of course; he knew she would lie. Why should she tell the truth, if his name had been used? If it had been, he would have to kill her. He —

He would find the record and destroy it and then, since he had killed once, he would kill again. Why shouldn't he? But first he would give her water. He would have to do that. He would —

But the steps did not, this time, come to the door of the bin. They started toward it; then veered away. They stopped. Then there was the harsh sound of something, apparently something heavy, being dragged on a cement floor. This lasted for a few moments and stopped. Then it began again, with a difference. Pam, who had at first listened dully, listened now with concentration. She got to her feet and, moving as softly as she could, went to the side of the bin nearest the sound and pressed close to the boards, listening.

Now, she thought, he was pulling the heavy thing up a flight of cement stairs. She could hear his breathing, and once a grunt of effort. Then that sound stopped. When sound started again, it was the screeching drag of something on level. This was very brief. Then there was the sound of a closing door.

There was an interval then of perhaps fifteen minutes before the next sound. It was of a door being opened and then closed; footsteps came after that, and this time came to the door of the bin. She turned to face the door, and the light glared at her.

"All right," the man whispered. "Come out!"

She did not move.

"Come out," he whispered again. "You'd better." There was threat in the whisper.

Pam North did as she was told. The light receded as she moved toward it, and she walked through the door. She took another step, saw dim light in a basement, saw an oil burner, thought, that's why the bin was empty, and then, from behind, something heavy, stifling, was over her head. It bore her down, it stifled her. Then she was pulled backwards.

It had been difficult to explain to Deputy Chief Inspector Artemus O'Malley. It was no easier to explain to the vigorous, youngish man with a crew haircut who sat across the desk; the man who said that he had no doubt whatever that Captain Weigand knew his business, but where did Hilda Godwin come into it? If he knew where she was, he would tell the captain,

65

naturally. His curiosity would remain.

"This burglar," Gilbert Rogers said, "gets killed. He's stolen a Voice-Scriber like that one" — he indicated — "from Hilda. I can see you want to give it back to her or, anyway, tell her where it is. But what's the rush?"

Bill Weigand looked reflectively at the Voice-Scriber on Mr. Rogers's desk. He did not see it; he nevertheless looked at it, as a platform speaker, improvising, may now and then look abstractedly at the ceiling. Youngish Mr. Rogers had, of course, put his finger on it. What was the rush?

There was an interruption. A trim and blond young woman came into the office and, seeing Weigand, said, "Oh" and prepared to leave. Rogers said, "Yes, Miss Agee?" and the blonde said, rather rapidly, "I'm sorry Mr. Forbush sent these in from Boston and said maybe you'd like to listen to them and you were out but I didn't know there was —"

"All right, Miss Agee," Rogers said. "Leave them. I'll listen to them."

Miss Agee put three square envelopes, one on top of the other, on Mr. Rogers's desk. She straightened the edges, making the pile neat. She went out. Bill Weigand looked abstractedly at the pile of stiff envelopes, not seeing them.

"Voice-Scriber records," Mr. Rogers said,

when Bill continued to look. "As I was saying —"

Bill saw the envelopes at which he had been looking — the squarish envelopes, each containing a recorded voice.

"They're mailed that way?" he asked.

"Sure," Rogers said. "Forbush up in the Boston office —" He stopped, because Bill Weigand did not seem to be listening. Bill reached out and picked up the topmost envelope. He read: "Do Not Bend." He read: "Voice-Scriber Record." A *squarish envelope*. Actually, a completely square envelope. Martha had said —

"Some authors dictate," Bill said. "Apparently Miss Godwin did?"

"She may have," Rogers said. His tone asked, "What difference does it make?" He considered. "I believe she did, now and then," he said. "You don't think your burglar stole a book? He didn't. We've got the book. At least, *a* book. I doubt whether she's started another. You can't tell about authors, of course." He sighed, perhaps at his own thoughts. He waited.

"We have to try to trace down every connection," Bill said. "Even connections as remote as this. We're looking for, talking to, everybody we can find who knew Harry Eaton. We're trying to find out where Eaton was yesterday, and the day before — who he saw, what he did, what he had for breakfast Sunday. Among other things, of course, we'd like to know when he broke into Miss Godwin's house. You see, we don't know what may turn out to be useful. Snappers-up of unconsidered trifles."

"Shakespeare," Mr. Rogers said. *"Winter's Tale,* I think. Hilda may be anywhere. Probably she is. She comes and she goes."

"So we were told," Bill said, and Gilbert Rogers said, "Um?"

"A man named Wilson," Bill told him. "Bernard Wilson. Tall, good looking, forty-odd."

"I know Wilson," Rogers said. "Damned near everybody knows Wilson. Creative writing at Dyckman, you know."

Bill shook his head.

"Professor of," Rogers told him. "Also critic, essayist, general consultant in the world of literature. And Rhodes Scholar. As a matter of fact, he gives us opinions now and then. He knew Hilda in the great days, you know. Where did you run into him?"

Bill explained where he had run into Professor Bernard Wilson. Rogers smiled. "Going to give her tea, was he?" he said. "That would interest her. Tea!"

Three-fourths of all questioning, perhaps of all conversation, is irrelevant, Bill Weigand thought. This, however, seemed to be going a

68

little far. Nevertheless, he repeated, "The great days?"

"The first fine careless rapture," Rogers said. He did not bother to identify. "Hilda's lyric life. About five years ago — that is, she started eight years ago when she was about seventeen. Very precocious. She kept at it until about four years ago, and stopped. Poetry, she thinks, is for the young. At twenty-one our Hilda decided she was outgrowing it."

"She was very good, I'm told," Bill said.

"She was wonderful, to put it simply," Rogers said. "In all ways, I'm told — I didn't know her in those days. Although —" He broke off.

"But you spoke of a book," Weigand said. "A book of hers you have. A collection?"

Rogers shook his head.

"A novel," he said. "She's taken to prose in — well, in what I suppose she thinks of as middle life."

"You people are going to publish it?" Bill asked.

"Oh, I think so," Rogers said. "It's the familiar first novel pattern, I'm told. I haven't had a go at it yet. I've been away. I'm told some of it is —" He broke off. He reminded Bill Weigand that they had been talking about burglary, not literature. "There is a difference," Gilbert Rogers added, with perhaps unnecessary firmness.

69

Weigand nodded. He asked if Rogers had known Miss Godwin long.

"About three years," Rogers said.

"Well?"

Rogers lifted his eyebrows. Weigand smiled faintly; he said he was thinking in connection with her possible whereabouts at the moment.

"Oh," Rogers said. "Well, she may have picked up and gone anywhere, as I said. If it were summer, I'd suggest the country – she's got a small place, not much more than a week-end place, up near South Salem. But that's closed up, now. Of course, she may be around town anywhere – you just started to look today, didn't you?"

"Right," Bill said. "No doubt she'll turn up at the house. We'll keep ringing."

"If she is in town," Rogers said, "I can tell you the most likely place to find her – at –" He looked at his watch. It seemed to surprise him. "About six," he said. "A little over half an hour from now." He looked pointedly at his desk, which was not clear. "Try the Four Corners. She'll drop in for a drink, probably. Even if she doesn't, her crowd will. You know Four Corners?"

Bill did. He apologized for the time he had taken. Rogers said it was nothing; he rose behind his desk. He was a big man; he might have been an amateur boxer at his university, which, from his speech, Bill Weigand took to have been Harvard. He gave Weigand a hard handshake to remember him by. "Come again any time," Rogers said. Harvard and Groton, Weigand thought, assuming precedent to be sound. Bill Weigand went from the large building of the Hudson Press and drove down Madison Avenue, and down Fifth, to the Village. He parked his car near the Four Corners Restaurant, and went to a telephone booth in a stationer's on the corner. He telephoned the Norths' apartment. Martha was still there. Mrs. North had not returned.

Bill went to the Four Corners, and into it, and to the handsome oval of the bar. He compared those already there with his memory of the publicity picture Gilbert Rogers had shown him. Hilda Godwin wasn't at the bar. Probably he was early.

He ordered scotch on the rocks from the nearest of four bartenders and, when it was poured, said, "Miss Godwin isn't around?" The bartender looked at a clock. "Little early yet," he said. "She —" He broke off. He said, "Evening, Professor," and Bill Weigand turned. Bernard Wilson said, "Evening, Harry" and started toward a group at the end of the bar before he saw Weigand. When he saw him he stopped, looked puzzled for a moment and then said, "Oh. Find her yet?"

"Not yet," Bill said. "And you?"

"No," Bernard Wilson said. "Not I." He half raised his hand in salute, and sauntered to join the group. Probably, Bill decided, it was Hilda Godwin's "crowd." He looked at it, sipping his drink.

The term "crowd" exaggerated. There had been four; now there were five. The arrival of Bernard Wilson upset the balance of sexes. The arrival of Wilson would also, in all probability, simplify Weigand's procedure. He sipped and waited; he thought about square envelopes which contained Voice-Scriber records; of a squarish envelope received by Pamela North and taken with her when she went. Went or, preposterously, was taken? From her own apartment? With no chance to cry out? Bill mentally shook his head.

Wilson was talking to the two men and two women he had joined. Both of the other men, sitting on bar stools, seemed to be tall men. Both were, Bill guessed, in their thirties. One was blond; he had a long, narrow head, sharp features and thin, expressive lips. The other was a dark man, his face square and ruddy, his shoulders heavy. They sat with the women between them. Nearest the dark man, as if by designed contrast, the woman had long hair, light red, curling to the shoulders of her green dress; nearest the sharp-faced man was a

72

woman whose hair was gray, but a kind of shining gray, molded in waves to a beautifully shaped head.

They offered movement when Wilson joined them, but he shook his head. He could not, his attitude indicated, stay; rearrangement would be a waste of time. The bartender brought him a drink he had evidently not needed to order; he drank a third of it and leaned along the bar to talk to the others. As he talked, the others looked at Weigand. The thin man shrugged to something Wilson said. Wilson turned toward Bill and motioned. Carrying his glass, Bill Weigand walked along the oval bar to them.

"I've been telling them about the burglary," Bernard Wilson said, in his carefully ordered voice. "That you are trying to find Hilda." He moved one well-shaped, large hand to identify "them." "They're all friends of Hilda's," he added.

"So you're a cop," the thin-faced man said, a British voice emphasizing, enjoying, familiarity with the quaintness of American argot. "I can't say you look it." He considered Weigand with a directness more often reserved for the inanimate. "Look like a gent," he remarked. "Doesn't he, Maddy?"

The girl with the reddish hair was a very pretty girl. She looked at Bill Weigand with the knowledge of her prettiness in her eyes.

73

"He has to try to be rude," she told Weigand. "He has to try very hard. Nobody pays any attention, of course."

"Darling," the thin-faced man said, and his flexible mouth smiled, twisted. Its movement was like a wink at Bill Weigand. "It's really no trouble, y' know."

"The speakers," Bernard Wilson said, "are, in order of appearance, Alec Lyster, who sometimes confuses himself with another Alec, and Miss Madeleine Barclay, who also acts." He then looked slightly embarrassed. He was afraid, he said, that he didn't remember the captain's name. Bill supplied it.

"He's investigating the burglary," Professor Wilson explained. The gray-haired woman joined by nodding her coiffed head.

"Hilda's gone south," the dark man said. "One of those places in Virginia, West Virginia — somewhere like that. Went Sunday."

He stopped. He lifted a glass and put it down. Bill Weigand slid onto a stool. He gave attention to the dark man.

"My name's Shaw," he said. "Garrett Shaw." He indicated the woman with the gray hair — with gray hair and a young face, clean jawline, smooth throat. "Mrs. Shaw. Alfrieda Shaw." He paused a moment; seemed to be waiting.

"I'm a sculptor," Mrs. Shaw said, in a voice as clear as glass. "Garry thinks everybody knows about it, Captain Weigand. Speak your piece, Garry."

"No piece," Garrett Shaw said. His voice was heavy. It almost rumbled. "Hilda had dinner with my wife and me Saturday night. I took her home after."

"Her errant footsteps," Alec Lyster said, in an aside, to nobody. "Shut up, Lyster," the red-haired girl said. "Let the man talk. Then you talk and then I'll talk and then —" Alec Lyster looked at her; his mouth winked at her. She quit talking.

"I'm interested in anything you can tell me, Mr. Shaw," Captain Weigand of the New York City police said, in character.

"If my bright young friends —" Shaw said. "I'll try to. Not that it's anything to tell." He looked at Weigand with sudden curiosity. "Come to think of it," he said, "haven't I heard of you? Read about you? Aren't you a homicide man?"

"Right," Bill said. "I am."

They all looked at him, then. There was surprise, and enquiry, on five faces.

"D'you mean something's wrong with Hilda?" Lyster asked. His voice was quick, sharp; it was as if he had, on the moment, come awake from a contented doze. The others waited. Bill Weigand shook his head.

"The man who broke into her house was

75

killed sometime Sunday night," Weigand said. "We're trying to trace his actions up to the time he was killed. Probably the murder had no connection with the burglary. There's no reason it should have had. The point is, we don't know when he broke into the house. It might help to know."

"Oh," Lyster said. "That's all it is?"

"Right," Bill said. "All I know of. Do you mind, Mr. Shaw?"

Shaw did not mind.

Hilda Godwin had dined with the Shaws Saturday night. There had been two other couples; the man they had invited for Hilda had, at the last moment, been unable to come. "Chap named Rogers," Shaw said. "Gilbert Rogers. With her publishers."

"I've met Mr. Rogers," Weigand said. He waited.

Around ten or so, one of the couples had left. "They've got kids and the baby sitter was running out," Shaw said. Half an hour or so later, the second couple had left.

"The three of us sat around and talked until – what time would you say, Frieda?"

"About midnight," Alfrieda Shaw said.

"Just about," her husband agreed. "So nothing would do but I take her home. The girl's been all over by herself, but I have to take her from Gramercy Park to Elm Lane."

"I thought it would be a nice thing to do," Alfrieda Shaw said, in her glass-clear voice.

"For me to do," Shaw said. "Anyway, I did. Took her home in a cab, helped her out of the cab, spread my coat over a mud puddle —"

"Really, Garry," Mrs. Shaw said.

"— carried her over the threshold, set her down in the hall, helped her off with her coat —"

"I wager you did, at that," Alec Lyster said. "You think, Frieda?"

Alfrieda Shaw was, lightly, sure of it.

"When you're all done," Shaw said, his deep voice rumbling.

"They're done, Garry," Madeleine Barclay said. "Such bright people."

"I intend," Lyster said, formally, "only the most innocent of malice. I am sure I speak for all of us."

Shaw sighed deeply. He waited; he waited a little longer than he needed.

"Hilda said she had a notion to go south," Shaw said, then. "Said she'd just had it. Then she said, 'You know, I think I will. Tomorrow. The Homestead or some place like that.' I said something or other — probably that it was a good idea, and that I wished Frieda and I could do the same. Then I left."

"This was in the hall?" Weigand asked.

"We may have stepped into the living room,"

77

Shaw said. "The hall's so small you damn near have to."

"And you didn't see any signs that the place had been broken into?" Weigand asked.

Shaw shook his square head.

"So far as you know, Miss Godwin didn't?"

Shaw was sure she hadn't. She hadn't, of course, had an opportunity to look around. They were talking; then he left.

"You didn't happen to notice whether there was a Voice-Scriber there?" Bill asked. "You know the device I mean?"

"Yes," Shaw said. "I didn't notice one way or another."

"Does any of you know where she works?" Bill asked. "I mean — in the living room? Upstairs? I've never been in the house, you know."

"Ground floor," Alec Lyster said. "Desk there, typewriter that dropped into the desk, y' know, this dictating thing on a table."

"I didn't see it," Shaw said. "I didn't notice one way or the other. If it had been stolen then — it was stolen?"

"Right," Bill said.

"— Hilda evidently didn't notice it while I was there," Shaw finished. "That's all I know about it."

"Right," Bill said. "Thank you, Mr. Shaw. We'll try to find Miss Godwin."

"I still don't see —" Shaw began.

"No," Bill said. "Well?" He looked around.

"I think," Lyster said, "that you have pumped us dry, Captain. Speaking of drought?"

Bill Weigand thanked him and said, "No." He had, he added, to be getting along.

"And so do I," Wilson said. "So do I."

Weigand paid and Bernard Wilson paid. They walked together to the door of the restaurant. Wilson said that he was afraid they hadn't helped particularly. "You hoped to find Miss Godwin there?" he added, as they stood outside. He had, Bill Weigand said, been told he might.

"Three evenings out of five, at least," Wilson said. "Lyster most evenings he's in town, usually with Madeleine. The Shaws, usually. Your friend Rogers drops in now and then; sometimes brings Hilda."

"Not my friend," Weigand said. "I met him this afternoon. Well — "

"He's quite taken with our Hilda, you know," Wilson said. "But then, so many are. And have been. Well, good evening, Captain."

He went off up the street, his topcoat neatly folded over his left arm. Bill Weigand went to his car. In it, he went to his office. He returned to neglected routine; he heard what there was to hear about Harry Eaton, which was considerable, but inconclusive. He had, apparently, been alive and reasonably well as late as Sunday afternoon; he lunched (hamburger and coffee) at a drugstore counter on Bleecker Street. During the late afternoon, he apparently had had visitors. One of them, the couple who had the flat next his thought, had been a woman. They had heard a woman talking, and a man they did not think was Eaton. They had not heard anything that was said.

There was a report that little Harry had had trouble with his landlord, but the landlord denied this. There was another rumor, harder to come by, more elusive, that he had been having trouble with a man known to be a fence (but not, as yet, provably so known) who, in turn, was believed to be connected with an outfit of heroin distributors. That might be interesting, if true.

Pam North had still not returned to her apartment. The alarm was out for her; the M.P.B. was making special efforts. Bill Weigand swore at that. He gave the Bureau the additional job of finding out, without a public alarm and if it could, where in the mid-south Hilda Godwin had gone.

She had not returned to her little house. Telephone calls had been made to it from time to time, and had gone unanswered. The patrolman on the beat was keeping an eye on the house, and had not been rewarded.

Bill Weigand summoned Mullins. He wanted

what could be discovered, quietly, about one Alec Lyster, apparently British, and one Garrett Shaw. Both frequenters of the Four Corners in Greenwich Village; one married to a sculptor, apparently well known; the other often with one Madeleine Barclay, apparently an actress. All four friends of Hilda Godwin. He would like to know, also, what could, without disturbing anyone's serenity, be found out about Professor Bernard Wilson of Dyckman University, and Gilbert Rogers, of the Hudson Press.

"O.K., Loot," Mullins said. But he raised heavy eyebrows and waited.

"To be quite honest, Mullins, I don't know," Bill told him. He drummed on his desk with his fingers.

"Mrs. North'll be O.K.," Mullins said. "She always is."

"Always has been," Weigand corrected. "I hope you're right."

Mullins went. Bill Weigand telephoned his wife and said he would be late. After a moment of hesitation, he told her why.

"Oh – *Bill!*" Dorian Weigand said. "Not Pam!"

"She'll be all right," Bill said. "She always is."

He went out for food he didn't want.

V

Tuesday, 10:40 P.M. to Wednesday, 1:25 A.M.

TWA Flight 36, the San Francisco Sky Chief, banked and turned, dropped toward lighted runways of La Guardia Airport. It touched down and rolled; it turned and taxied back. Gerald North was one of the first out of the Constellation. He found a telephone booth and dialed, and waited. He heard the signal of the telephone ringing. He heard it for a long time, but it did not stop. He dialed another number, and it was quickly answered.

But Bill Weigand was not there. Mullins was not there. Jerry talked to Sergeant Stein.

"Nothing yet," Stein said. "She'll be all right, Mr. North. We'll find her."

"Yes," Jerry said. "Sure."

But it wasn't yes. It wasn't sure. He got a taxicab and gave an address. "Make it as fast as you can," he told the driver. "Sure," the driver said, "fast as I can, bud." But the cab crept to the Triborough, crept down the east side. In front of the apartment house, Jerry gave the driver a bill. "Hey, bud," the driver said after

82

him, but not in a tone that insisted he be heard. In a hurry to keep his date, bud was — in five dollars' worth of hurry.

There was no date, except with the cats. They greeted him, were at first ignored. They protested loudly; they followed Jerry North — a friend turned strange, paying no attention to cats — from room to room. Finally Jerry looked at them.

"Damn you," Jerry said. "Why can't you talk? You were here. Why can't you talk?"

They talked enough. It did no good.

Across a continent, Jerry North had driven a great plane with his urgency. In Chicago, while the plane fueled, he had walked back and forth, back and forth, lighting, dragging at, stepping on, cigarettes. When the plane was again in the air, he drove it on.

He would get home. He would find Pam. She would be in the apartment, waiting. He had only to get there. If she were not there — *but she would be, had to be* — he would find her. He would know what to do, where to look. It would be all right, once he was home again.

But the apartment was strange. Familiar chairs, familiar sofas were strange, not his — not anybody's. He was a man who had run across a continent, and run to nothingness. Jerry North sat suddenly in a chair by the telephone. He lighted a cigarette, not noticing he did so. Strange cats sat in a circle around him, staring through cats' flat eyes.

He dialed again. Captain Weigand was still out. He would be told Mr. North had called. Mullins was out. Sergeant Stein had gone off duty.

"All right," Jerry North said, dully. "I'll call again."

He put the receiver back in the cradle. The bell under it rang shrilly. Jerry's left hand leaped to the telephone. Suddenly, he had too little breath to speak with. He said, "Yes?"

It was not Pam. The voice was a man's, heavy, unfamiliar.

"Mr. North?" the voice said.

"Yes."

"This is Helder," the voice said. "Sven Helder. You know? At the building."

"Yes," Jerry said. "What is it, Helder?"

"I got to wondering," Helder said. "Mrs. North got home all right last night?"

"What?" Jerry said. His voice was quick again.

"Mrs. North," Helder said. "She was here last night. Up at your office. She got home all right, didn't she?"

"She was there?" Jerry said. "At the office? No — she didn't get home all right. We're trying to find her."

There was a brief pause.

"Well," Helder said, "she was here and she left all right. Anyway, I thought – I tell you how it was. I got worried. She was –"

"Wait!" Jerry said. "You're there now?"

"Sure," Helder said.

"Stay there," Jerry told him. "I'm coming up. You'll stay there?"

"Sure," Helder said. "I got to, anyway. I got –"

Jerry North did not wait. He cradled the telephone. He went hatless, without a coat. He thought an empty cab would never come along Sixth Avenue. But one came.

The glass doors of the building were closed. There was a dim light in the lobby. Jerry put a finger on the night bell and held it there. Sven Helder came through the lobby, lifting a suspender strap over his shoulder. He peered through the glass. He nodded. He took keys from his pocket, slowly. He selected a key; he peered at it and shook his head. He turned the bunch of keys slowly in his hands and chose another. To this one, unhurriedly, he nodded. Finally, he opened the doors.

He talked as slowly as he had moved. Jerry had to hold tight to himself, force himself to wait. He got the story.

Pam had come to the building at nine-thirty Monday night – 9:32, exactly, by Helder's watch. He took the watch from his pocket and showed it to Jerry North, and nodded at it, and put it back. He had taken her upstairs. At ten-thirty, when it was time to lock the building for the night, she had not come down. He went up then and found the offices dark, and knew she had left, walking down. He had locked up after her, checked that she had not signed out, grumbled a little about it.

"Only today, I got to worrying," he said. "You know how women is. Just as likely to forget to sign out as remember. Regulations, but what do they care? But then I got to thinking – I never know Mrs. North be like that. Thinks about other people, know what I mean? So I thought tonight I'd just call up and see if she was all right, and you say she didn't get home. So –"

"Let's go up," Jerry said.

They went, in the reluctantly trundling elevator. Again, Jerry fought slowness; again he felt a desperate need to be in time.

But when the lights were on in the offices, it was again as it had been. There was only emptiness; only, again, the disturbing strangeness of familiar things.

Pam had come here Monday night – come to this place of empty desks. She had been here – how long? She had come here – why?

The lights glared down on the empty general office, revealing everything and nothing. As

86

much as out of habit as for any reason, Jerry went to his own corner office, and Helder followed him. The lights there revealed only the flat surfaces of familiar things – revealed a cleared desk, a Voice-Scriber on a small, wheeled table, chairs and a telephone and two walls of books. Here – almost certainly here, to this office – Pam had come at about nine-thirty the evening before. She had been here; she had touched these chairs, this desk. Had she opened and closed again the small, personal file beside the desk? Had she put something in, or taken something out?

He sat at the desk; he looked at the memo calendar on it. Tuesday, October 28, the calendar assured him. When Pam was there, it had said Monday, October 27. Miss Corning had dusted the desk, torn off yesterday. Abstractedly, Jerry North tore Tuesday off. He examined drawers, not knowing what he sought in them, and found nothing that spoke of Pam. He pulled out the upper drawer of the filing cabinet and looked at it, but did not begin to search it. He could spend hours doing that, with no certainty of gain. He pushed it closed again.

"She didn't say why she came?" he asked Helder. "You're sure she didn't?"

"Why would she tell me?" Helder asked. "No, she didn't say."

"Was she carrying anything?" Jerry asked. "A package?"

"Just one of these bags they carry," Helder said. He used the word "they" in reference to strange creatures, inexplicable creatures. It was in his tone. "She wasn't wearing any hat, though," he added.

"She doesn't, much," Jerry said. "She —" He stopped.

(She bought hats; she often bought hats. She wore each hat once or twice, and not again. "Maybe I've sort of outgrown hats," Pam North said. Her voice filled the room. "They always begin to look silly," Pam North said.)

"What?" Jerry said, to the other voice — the heavy, real voice — in the room. "What did you say?"

"When she put them down to sign in," Helder said.

"Put what down?"

"With her purse," Helder said. "I remember now. She put it down to sign in and there was something under it. An envelope, like. A square envelope."

Jerry was back, by then. His questions were quick, but the answers were slower. Just a square envelope, under the purse. That was all he could remember. Pam had brought a square envelope with her to the office; whether she had taken it with her when she left, there was no way of knowing. It was something to look for. Jerry looked. He found square envelopes – large envelopes for unfolded manuscript sheets (not square, but near enough); square envelopes for Voice-Scriber records. (There was a box of these; they were almost never used. They were empty.)

"That looks about right," Helder said, of the Voice-Scriber envelope. "A little bigger, maybe. But I don't know."

Jerry North needed help – professional help. He lifted the telephone on his desk and listened for a second to its deadness before he remembered. He went then to the switchboard at the receptionist's desk. He dialed, holding one earpiece of the headset to his ear. The answer was not so quick, this time. It came in a weary voice. But it was the right answer – "Weigand speaking." Then Jerry North talked fast.

"She had an envelope?" Bill said. "About the size and shape of a record envelope? Wait, then. I'll be up."

He was, in a surprisingly short time; Mullins with him. Bill looked at Jerry North. He said, "She'll be all right. We'll find her."

"Sure," Jerry said. "Sure she'll be all right."

To Bill's quick questions, Helder could give them little more than he had already given. One thing, yes. The offices had been cleaned since Mrs. North was there. They were cleaned every night, between six and eight. Bill Weigand swore at that. "Let's hope they gave it a lick and a promise," he said. "Come on, Mullins."

The policemen worked together, dusting gray powder, blowing it away. They dusted the office; the washroom adjoining it; even the sill of the window which opened on a fire escape. As they worked, Bill Weigand talked. He told Jerry of little Harry Eaton; of Hilda Godwin. He asked questions.

Hilda Godwin, Jerry knew of; had met once or twice. He had heard she was writing a novel. He had not been much interested, since it would, naturally, go to her usual publishers — the Hudson Press. Eaton he did not remember. Then he remembered Eaton's book.

"God awful," he said. "Somebody read it. I only looked at a couple of pages. That was plenty."

"You never met him?" Weigand asked, blowing dust from the surface of the Voice-Scriber.

Jerry hadn't. But then he remembered something else: with the manuscript, there had been a letter from Eaton. Eaton had thought Mr. North might like "My Life in Crime" because Mr. North knew about things like that, being a "kind of detective." Jerry remembered the phrase; he heard it or its equivalent too frequently.

90

"Right," Bill said. "Mullins!"

Mullins turned from the filing case.

"Here," Bill Weigand said. "Let's see the blow-up."

They both looked, then. They looked from the blown-up photograph of Pam North's fingerprints to whorls in gray dust, and back again.

"O.K., Loot," Mullins said. "That's it."

They kept at it; they found other of Pam North's prints. One set under the edge of the desk top — a set of four fingers of her left hand, as if she had hooked her fingers there, standing in front of it. Several individual prints on the Voice-Scriber.

When they had finished, Bill Weigand stood for a minute or more and looked at nothing.

"It could be this way," he said, then. He spoke slowly. "Eaton steals a Voice-Scriber, planning to hock it. He finds a record on it and plays the record back. Something he hears — well, we can't guess. Say it worried him. He didn't want to come to us, naturally. He doesn't want anything to do with us. So — he sent the record to you. I don't know how he'd happen to have an envelope."

"In the case," Jerry said. "The carrying case. There's a compartment for them."

"Right," Bill said. "He mailed it to you. Pam opened it. Probably thought it was addressed to

91

her. I've seen Eaton's writing. It's a scrawl. She brought it here and played it. But somebody —" He stopped, then. He looked at Jerry.

"Somebody killed Eaton," Jerry said.

"Listen," Bill said, "we don't know this was why, do we?"

"For God's sake, Bill!" Jerry said.

"Take it easy," Bill said. "Take it easy, fella. We don't know. Pam'll be all right."

"Sure," Jerry said. His voice was dull. He sat down suddenly. "I was out in San Francisco," he said. "I was at a party. Listen, Bill — *I was at a party.*"

"Snap out of it!" Bill Weigand said.

"Sure," Jerry said. "Sure, Bill. I'll snap out of it." He sat and looked at nothing. His fists clenched. He raised them a few inches, and brought them down again. Then, suddenly, he stood up.

"Why don't we do something?" he demanded. "Why the hell?"

"Listen," Bill said. "Get yourself together. *Listen!* We'll do something."

Jerry North looked at him, not seeming to see him. He spoke dully. "There's no place to start," he said.

There was, Bill told him. If he'd snap out of it, he'd see the place to start.

"What?" Jerry said.

He was told to think.

"Hilda Godwin's," Jerry said. "It started there."

"Right," Bill Weigand said. "You're damned right."

The three of them went down in the slowly creaking elevator. They waited while Helder unlocked the front doors. As they crossed to the police car, they heard him lock the doors again. They went downtown, fast, to the little house in Elm Lane.

"Listen, Loot," Mullins said. "We got no warrant."

"No," Bill said. "We haven't, have we?"

"O.K.," Mullins said. "I just mentioned it."

The little house was dark. But it was after midnight, then. It was a time for houses to be dark. They rang the bell at the top of the short flight of immaculate white stairs. They rang it again.

"I'll tell you, Loot," Mullins said. "The back would be better, sort of."

"Right," Bill said. Absently, he fingered the knob of the door. It turned in his fingers. "The front'll do," Bill Weigand said. He opened the door, slowly, quietly. The three of them went into the little house.

The hall was almost too small for three men. Entering it, they faced a narrow flight of stairs, leading to the second floor. At their right was an opening, the width of double doors.

93

Through it – and they went through it, Mullins's flashlight beam showing the way – was the living room. It was about ten feet in width. It ran the depth of the little house. It was almost a hall, in dimensions; it was a most glorified hall. Weigand pressed a tumbler switch near the door and light came on in a small, ornate, yet oddly beautiful, chandelier midway of the room. Light reflected from cut crystals. The light fell on heavy, deep red, curtains looped at the windows at either end, down one side, of the long, narrow room. It fell on Victorian chairs and sofas; on the marble mantel of a small fireplace at the far end of the room, on a mirror above the mantel and an intricate, small white clock on the mantel shelf. The light fell on white woodwork; on wall paper intricately patterned in gold. The room was perfect in its recreation of another day – a more opulent day.

Mullins whistled, softly.

The room was empty. They could see that immediately the lights were on. They went through it, nevertheless. At the rear of the room, on the left, a sliding door hid a small kitchen, which was by no means Victorian. It, too, was empty. They went back through the room and up the stairs. At the top of the stairs they found a bathroom, a very narrow hall and two bedrooms.

The bedroom at the rear was, evidently, Hilda Godwin's. It was small, but not too small for a canopied bed; not too small for a vanity made of mirrors, but wearing skirts. There were crystal sconces on either side of the dressing table. It was a little like the inside of a jewel box, but the single window at the rear was fitted with an air-conditioning unit. The other bedroom, which inter-communicated but could also be reached from the narrow hall, was more matter of fact. It did not, as the rear bedroom did, have the atmosphere of frequent occupancy.

Both rooms were empty. In each, the beds were neatly made. The closet off the front bedroom held some summer dresses; the larger closet of the rear bedroom was filled with clothes — pretty clothes, very modern clothes.

Nowhere, on the second floor or on the floor below, was there anything to indicate that violence, or even precipitate action, had occurred in the little house. They went back down again. And, again, Jerry North felt that they had hurried, had run, to nothingness.

They went over the living room more carefully the second time. The desk at which, they could assume, Hilda Godwin worked, was Victorian in external design, modern in convenience. A typewriter emerged from it, smoothly, when the proper knob was pulled.

"Missed that, Eaton did," Mullins commented. "Maybe he was in a hurry."

But there was no sign Eaton had been there at all. If he had, in searching for objects at once of value and portable, disturbed the room's other-day elegance, evidence of his marauding had been smoothed away. It was Mullins who found, pushed into a corner, partly under bookshelves, a small, wheeled table. It was Jerry who, before the others, recognized it.

"That's where she kept the Voice-Scriber," he said. His voice was dull.

Looking at it closely, with the beam of Mullins's torch lighting it obliquely, they could see the outline, faint in just perceptible dust, of the device Eaton had stolen. They confirmed what they already knew. They stood for a moment and looked at the little table, and the sound they heard, although a small sound, was loud in the room.

"The basement!" Bill Weigand said, quickly, his voice low.

They had missed it the first time; they found it quickly. The door opened off the little kitchen; it opened on a steep flight of wooden stairs. The beam from the torch knifed down the stair flight. Bill Weigand's voice traveled down the beam of light, as flat, as without inflection, as the light itself.

"All right," Weigand said. "Come up."

For a moment there was silence. Then there was a sound of movement. Then a tall, youngish man, with a crew haircut, stood in the beam of light. He held a flashlight of his own, turned off. He looked up into the glare.

"All right, Mr. Rogers," Bill Weigand said. "Come up."

For a moment, Gilbert Rogers, associate editor of the Hudson Press, blinked in the light. Then he came up. They moved back to let him through the kitchen, into the living room.

"Well?" Bill Weigand said.

"So it's you," Rogers said. He looked at the others. "Hello, Rogers," Jerry North said.

"What the hell goes on?" Rogers asked them.

"Perhaps you'd better tell us," Bill Weigand said.

Rogers hesitated.

"Now," Weigand advised.

Rogers looked from one to the other of the three men. He looked longest at Jerry North, and then seemed most puzzled. He looked back at Bill Weigand.

"I got worried," he said. "After you left — something came up. I got worried about Hilda."

"Why?" Bill asked him. "You weren't this afternoon, Mr. Rogers. Why are you now?"

Rogers hesitated again. They waited.

"Well," he said, "the manuscript I was telling

you about – the manuscript of her novel – it's disappeared. I found that out after you left. I decided to take it home and start reading it. And – we seem to have lost it. First Miss Godwin goes away, without telling anybody –"

He stopped, because Weigand was shaking his head.

"She told a man named Shaw," he said. "Told him that she was going south. That –"

"What's Shaw got to do with it?" Rogers demanded. He flushed a little; his words were hurried. "Where does he come into it?"

Bill Weigand told him. Rogers shook his head, with violence. They waited.

"Maybe she told him that," Rogers said. "Maybe she thought of going. But she didn't go. She'd have told me before she went." He spoke with conviction.

"Why?" Bill asked.

"Because –" Rogers began, and hesitated, and went on more slowly. "She's submitted this book," he said. "We hadn't made a decision on it. She wouldn't go away without telling us where we could reach her." He looked at Jerry. "You know that, North," he said. Jerry nodded.

"You didn't mention that this afternoon," Bill said. "You seemed to think it was perfectly reasonable that she should merely go off somewhere."

"I know," Rogers said. "It's true, she does do

that. But then, I got to thinking. And then the business about the manuscript came up."

"Go ahead," Weigand said. "Tell us about that, Mr. Rogers."

Rogers told them. The manuscript of Hilda Godwin's novel had come in, from her agent, about two weeks before. At that time, Rogers, who normally would have read it first, was away on vacation. "I've been her contact at the office recently," Rogers explained. "Not on much — reprints of her earlier stuff, that sort of thing. Mr. Wilmot felt that, since the editor she used to work with isn't with us any more, I might as well handle her prose, if she was going in for prose." But with Rogers away, a preliminary reader had gone over the book and then it had been started on the rounds of advisory readers. "Just to get things moving," Rogers explained. "In the end, I'd have made the recommendation to Mr. Wilmot, and he'd have decided. But with her name —" He shrugged, and looked at Jerry North. Jerry nodded.

The first advisory reader had recommended publication, although he had qualified his approval. In some respects, it was a characteristic first novel. It was obviously autobiographical. Then it had gone to Professor Bernard Wilson. He had returned the manuscript a few days earlier. "Last Friday," Rogers said. It had not been seen since.

Wilson had personally returned the manuscript, leaving it with the receptionist in the outer office. He had also brought along his report, in a separate envelope. The receptionist had given him a receipt for the manuscript and put it on her desk, along with the report. "He's very enthusiastic about the book," Rogers added.

This was in the middle of the afternoon. The receptionist was busy; the afternoon was busy. She had left her desk frequently to announce the more important of the visitors. It was late in the afternoon that she noticed the manuscript was missing, although the envelope containing Wilson's favorable report was still on the desk.

"And, reasonably enough, she supposed somebody had picked it up," Rogers said. "One of our people, I mean. She was so sure that she didn't even mention it until Monday. It took most of Monday to find out that none of us had taken it. So —" He shrugged. "The point is," he said, "nobody steals a manuscript. What would be the point?"

Nevertheless, somebody had taken, if "stolen" was too strong a word, the manuscript of Hilda Godwin's novel.

"I didn't hear of it until late this afternoon, as I said," Rogers told them. "And then — then I got worried. I kept trying to reach Hil – Miss Godwin and finally I came down here. She didn't answer so – well, I found the door was unlocked. I came in and called her a couple of times and then started to look around." He looked around now, from Bill Weigand to Jerry North to Sergeant Aloysius Mullins. His expression suggested they make something of it.

"For another copy of the typescript?" Jerry suggested.

"For that," Rogers said. "For Hilda herself. For anything I could find. I was worried."

"About the manuscript?" Bill suggested. There was a certain note in his voice. Rogers looked at him.

"All right," he said. "About Hilda. It's nobody's business but ours, but we're –" he hesitated momentarily – "planning to get married. That's really why I know she didn't go south without telling me. I know she's all right, of course but –" He let it hang.

"You're sure the door was unlocked when you came?" Bill Weigand asked. "That you came here, just on a chance, and just happened to find the door unlocked?"

He waited; he very obviously waited, very skeptically waited. After a moment the tall, youngish man flushed again.

"All right," he said. "I've got a key. I didn't say so because you'd misunderstand. It's –

Hilda and I are going to get married."

"Right," Bill said. "You told us that. Well – did you find anything here? In the basement, say?"

"I just started there," Rogers said. "I looked down here, then upstairs. For her copy of the manuscript, I mean. She has a filing case down in the basement for old manuscripts and I was looking there. Then I heard you come in and –"

"Decided to wait us out," Bill told him.

"All right," Rogers said. "But I got cramped and moved and hit a box or something."

"Although for all you knew we might have been anybody," Bill said. "A new set of burglars. Or – Miss Godwin and some friends. Mr. Shaw, say, or –"

"All right," Rogers said. "I listened. I wanted to find out. There's an air shaft or something and it's easy to listen. If Shaw had been here, I'd have come up fast enough." He made the last statement with peculiar vigor.

"Why?" Weigand asked him.

"Because the –" he began. He stopped. "Never mind," he said.

They waited.

"He won't leave her alone," Rogers said, after the silence had gone on, pressed down on him. "He keeps – bothering her. His wife knows it; everybody knows it. He's not – not

102

rational about it. She's told him no, she's told him about us. It doesn't do any good. I'm about ready —" He stopped again.

"I wouldn't," Bill said.

Jerry North had had enough, by then.

"For God's sake, Bill," he said. "Can't you let this slide? We've got to —"

"Right," Bill said. "You didn't find anything in the basement?"

The last was to Rogers. Rogers shook his head.

"We'll try again," Bill said. "You too, Mr. Rogers." It was more order than invitation. They went back to the steep flight of wooden stairs, found a light switch at the top of it, went down into a cellar dimly lighted by a single dangling bulb. The flashlights helped.

There was an oil burner; there was a filing cabinet, as Rogers had said. It was dust covered; the dust was smeared. "Let's see your hands, Mr. Rogers," Weigand said, and looked at them under the flashlight beam. They were grimed. They bore out his story.

"Look for it," Weigand said. "Mullins will help."

Rogers hesitated a moment, turned to the filing cabinet; opened the top drawer and began to go through papers, bound typescripts. Mullins helped by watching.

The basement was small, like the house. At

the far end, a short flight of cement stairs ran up to a padlocked door.

Opposite the oil burner there was a relic of the past — a coal bin of rough, heavy boards, built out into the basement. The door was closed. They looked there first, by flashlight. There was coal dust on the floor, but it did not lie evenly. Feet had scuffed it; here something, or someone, had lain on the floor.

Jerry saw the handkerchief first. It was small and black with dust. It had been white; it had had a brown border. Jerry North picked it up. As he held it, his hands shook a little.

"Pam had one like this," he said. "She wore it in the pocket of her dress. A beige wool dress." He lifted the handkerchief to his face. "I think it's the scent she uses," he said. His voice was dull.

"It's not there," Rogers said behind them and, behind him, Sergeant Mullins said, "That's right, Loot."

Jerry and Bill Weigand hardly heard them.

"She'll be all right," Bill Weigand said.

"Look," Jerry said. "Would you just as soon stop saying that?"

They looked further. It did not take them long. At the end of the basement nearest the flight of cement steps there were several trunks and boxes. There had been one more, trunk or box. It was outlined on the floor; the marks of its dragged movement to and up the steps was clear. The marks stopped at the padlocked door.

Jerry North wrenched at the door with his hands, fruitlessly. Bill stopped him. He sent Mullins to the police car for a tool.

"Wait, Mr. Rogers," Bill said, when Rogers moved as if to follow Mullins.

VI

Wednesday, October 29: 1:27 A.M. to 4:15 A.M.

The area behind Hilda Godwin's little house was surrounded by a high board fence. The yard was the width of the house itself, and rather longer. The center section was paved; between pavement and fence there was a border of earth, cleaned now and raked smooth; clearly in summer a border of such flowers as could be brought to live in the city of New York. Near the door through which Jerry North led the way after the padlock had been wrenched from it, was a pile of summer furniture, covered by a tarpaulin. There was nothing under the tarpaulin except summer furniture.

The flashlights played around the yard. They followed the fence from its juncture with the house, along the side which shut off the street, across, and up to the house again. On the street side, midway down, there were double doors, closed. At the doors, the strip of earth ended and pavement took its place; beyond the doors, the strip again resumed.

"She keeps her car in here a lot of the time,"

Rogers said. "A station wagon. It isn't here."

It wasn't there. Opposite the double doors, drip from a car had stained the cement.

"She leaves it there," Rogers said, needlessly. He pointed. "Packs it up for the country and —" He stopped. *"That's where she's gone,"* he said. "Up to the country. She filled the trunk, dragged it out here and put it in the car and —" Again he stopped.

"By herself?" Weigand asked.

"All right," Rogers said. "Somebody helped her." He turned suddenly. "Look," he said, "you aren't keeping me here all night. Do you want to charge me with anything?"

"Charge you?" Weigand repeated. "With what, Mr. Rogers? You had a key, you say. Given you by Miss Godwin. What would I charge you with?"

"Then I'm getting out of here," Rogers said. "If she's gone up there with —" He broke off. "You can do what you want," he said.

"Rogers!" Jerry said. "Listen! I think my wife was here. Was — held here. What do you know about this?" He moved toward Rogers; Rogers was the larger man, but he drew back.

"Hold it, Jerry," Bill said. He moved forward. Jerry North stopped and turned, and shook his head slowly. "She was here," he said.

"Right," Bill said. "I think she was. And — wasn't hurt here. There's no sign of that. She's

107

probably gone with Miss Godwin wherever —"

"Up to the country," Rogers said. "I keep telling you."

"You know where it is?" Jerry asked. "This place of hers?"

"Yes," Rogers said. "Of course. Up beyond South Salem. On a back road."

Jerry turned to Bill.

"Right," Bill Weigand said. "We'll get going. You've got a car, Mr. Rogers?"

Rogers had. It was parked in Elm Lane.

"Take Sergeant Mullins with you," Weigand said. "We'll follow."

Rogers seemed to hesitate for a moment. Then he said, "All right."

They went too fast through unfrequented streets; they went up a ramp at Nineteenth Street to the West Side Highway, and then far too fast north on the Henry Hudson Parkway and the Saw Mill River Road. At the Cross County Parkway turnoff, Rogers's Oldsmobile hesitated, but then went on north on the Saw Mill. Only at the Hawthorne Circle did it turn right, ignoring the stop sign, its tires squealing on the turn.

They left White Plains behind and raced north and east on Route 22, which was wide at first and then narrowed, turned often. Rogers took chances on the bends; the police car clung behind the Olds. "He's quite a driver," Bill

108

Weigand said. "Poor Mullins."

Jerry North said nothing. You ran and ran — across a continent, through city streets, now on country roads. You came to nothing in the end.

Beyond Bedford Village they turned sharp right and, miles — but only minutes — later they turned right again at Cross River. Minutes more, and the sleeping village of South Salem was behind them; they were on a back road, gravel spurting under tires; they were climbing. Stop lights blared red in front of the police car, then, and the Olds twisted from the road. When they reached the place, there was a lane there, and the tail lights of the other car ahead still, and still climbing. The Olds led them through a gap in a stone wall and stopped on a driveway.

Hilda Godwin's other house seemed large; under the lights of the two cars, it rambled along a ridge. It was of brown shingles, in part two-storied. It was dark. On the drive there was no other car. The doors of the garage stood open, and the garage was empty. As they walked toward the house from the cars, they kicked through the fallen leaves of autumn.

Weigand knocked on the door Rogers led them to, but knocking was a formality. This door, too, was unlocked when he tried the knob. Inside, the torch beams lighted a square hall. In the center of the hall there was a square trunk – a large trunk, a new one.

"There it is," Rogers said. "I remember it. She decided to come up here and – *Hilda! Hey! Where are you?*" He shouted the last. His voice echoed in the hall; must have echoed through the house; was not answered. Rogers started to call again, but his voice trailed to silence. He stood and looked at the trunk.

"All right, Mullins," Bill Weigand said. "Open it."

Mullins was prepared, now. Steel wrenched at the trunk lock; metal protested harshly. The tongue of the lock bent back. Mullins looked down at the trunk, and hesitated.

"You may as well go ahead," Weigand said, his voice quiet. He reached out and grasped an arm of Jerry North, who stood beside him. "Go ahead, Mullins."

Mullins lifted the lid.

The body was doubled up in the trunk. Jerry North's breath went out, shudderingly.

It was a small body. The face might have been delicate once, quick with expression. The body might have been light and gay under the yellow dinner dress.

Rogers turned away, his face working; he made a strange, meaningless sound – a sick sound.

"Put it down, Mullins," Bill Weigand said,

his voice without expression. "Miss Godwin's been dead several days, I'm afraid."

Rogers made the same sick sound again. He turned from the trunk; he seemed to see no one. He seemed to grope his way to the door, and out into the night.

Mullins lowered the trunk lid. He swore, softly.

"Of course," Weigand said, "we had to expect it. Even so —"

"It's what Pam — knew about, isn't it?" Jerry said. He mumbled the words a little.

"Probably," Weigand said. "It shaped that way, you know. We had —"

He stopped as, outside, the engine of a car came suddenly, harshly, to life. He turned, and then ran toward the door. Mullins ran after him.

They shouted at the turning Oldsmobile, and ran toward it. But Rogers did not stop. The car cut off the drive, lurched for a moment on turf, through fallen leaves, came out of the turn, kicking dirt and gravel behind it. It was through the gap, then. Mullins ran toward the police car.

"No!" Bill said sharply. "Let him go, Sergeant."

Mullins stopped; he came back.

"See if the telephone's connected," Bill Weigand told him. "Get the State Police, if it is.

111

Then the office. Get things started."

"Pickup on Rogers?" Mullins said.

"Right," Bill told him. "And – tell them they'd better put a couple of men on Shaw."

"Oh," Mullins said. He tried again. "O.K., Loot," Sergeant Mullins said.

Jerry was already searching the rambling house; already calling, "Pam! Pam!"

Nobody answered. They found nobody.

The State Police found nobody when they came, with sirens – then with lights, with photographers, with the paraphernalia of fingerprinting.

"She was strangled, I think," Bill Weigand told the sergeant in charge. The sergeant thought so, too.

Outside the house, behind it, where a garden had been, they found the start of a hole. It would have been a rather large hole – larger than an ordinary grave. But it was too shallow for a grave.

If the hole had been planned as a grave, and dug deeper, it would easily have held two bodies, particularly if neither was large.

It had all the quality of a nightmare – the shifting, distorted shape of a nightmare; the unreasonableness of a nightmare. It was the unreasonableness, more even than the simple physical danger, which was obvious

112

even while it was unbelievable, that caused a kind of screaming in Pamela North's mind. She had been in trouble before, thanks in large measure to having met, years ago, a policeman attached to Homicide. But the trouble, while never really expected, had grown logically out of something in which she, along with Jerry, had got herself involved. This was different. This time, Pam North told her screaming mind, I didn't *do* anything.

She was in a woods, apparently on top of a hill. There were tall trees around her and most of them had lost their leaves. They reached black, twisted branches toward a sky across which the clouds hurried through the light of a small, a quite inadequate, moon. She was, sometime in the middle of the night, lost in the woods somewhere − but she had no real idea where − in the vicinity of New York. She unquestionably was, although there was now no sign of it, being pursued by a whispering man who could, if logic meant anything, exist only in a nightmare, but who had very tangibly existed in the most common place of surroundings − a deserted office late in the evening. Pam shook her head, which still ached. She stood and looked around her, and wondered where she was. She wished the trees more friendly.

Her escape − if she had actually escaped; in

a nightmare it was difficult to be sure — had been of a part with the rest. The whispering man had bungled, as he must have bungled from the beginning, and not only because murder is always a bungle. If any of all this meant anything, had any logic, he had killed while a machine listened and recorded, and had not had the competence to discover this until too late. (How he had discovered it then she could only guess.) Then he had — well, then he had behaved like a man in a nightmare, like a man gone berserk. He had, for one thing, put a preposterous value on the recording, which did not —

Pam, standing still in the middle of a woods, on a hilltop, stopped herself there. There was no point in making the whispering man out more of a bungler than he really was. The recorded dialogue between murderer and victim did not, to be sure, identify either. But — the murderer had not had the record. If he had got his hands on it, he would have destroyed it. Therefore, he had not heard it. Therefore, he did not know what was on it; could not remember now what he had said, and what the woman had said. Obviously, he could not remember whether names had been used. Under those circumstances, getting his hands on the record, and destroying it, would seem vital. Once you granted that —

The way he had gone about it remained, however, the way of a man lunging in the dark. It was, Pam thought, as if his first act had unstrung the man; since his first act had been murder, done in a moment of fury, that was not unreasonable, given a certain kind of man — given, say, a man unused to stress, unaccustomed to planning, to testing, to looking ahead. Such a man might very well lunge, as if in the dark, doing without further consideration what first came into his head. Granted that all murderers are unbalanced, this one — who might even now be approaching her through the trees — had a further characteristic: he was inexperienced. This did not help; a hand grenade is at its most dangerous, to everybody, in inexperienced hands.

These thoughts were a jumble in Pam North's mind. When she had got so far with logic, she gave it up and began to hurry, almost to run, through the trees. She started down the hill, hoping she was putting more distance between herself and the house from which she had escaped, but by no means sure of it. She had been doing that now for, she guessed, several hours.

She had been taken to the house, tied up, under a blanket, on the floor of a station wagon. Once there, she had been locked up in a room on the second floor — a room with one window. Left there, without comment even in a whisper, she had eventually got the window open. It was only on the second floor, but on this side of the house the ground dropped precipitously, so that the distance to it was as great as it might have been if she had been a story higher in the house. That was no good, unless she had to decide between broken legs and a broken neck.

She had heard him moving around below; she had heard him dragging into the house a trunk with which she had shared the station wagon. She had a sick feeling that she knew what was in the trunk. She had heard the man go out of the house again and for a long time had heard nothing further. Then she had heard the motor of a car, presumably the station wagon, start up. She had tried the door then, careless of the noise she made, but quickly found it beyond her. She had tried another door, which she had supposed led merely to a closet, and found that she had been right. It was on her third hopeless check of her surroundings that she discovered a trap door in the ceiling of the closet.

Standing on a chair, she pushed up against the trap door, having little hope. It was preposterously easy to open; suspiciously easy to open. He had seemed to know the house. Surely he would not have put her in a room from which, with no more effort than this, she might get out. She hesitated; presumably the trap door, even if she could clamber up through it, would lead her merely to a new, less comfortable, confinement. But she thought: knowing a house well enough does not mean you know all the odd things about it, particularly if it is an old house. She pushed aside the trap door, which was unhinged, and tried to climb.

She failed twice. She broke fingernails. Dust poured down, blindingly. She tried a third time, and pulled herself partly up. Her legs waved wildly; the edge of the flooring cut into her bruisingly. Then she got one foot on the top of the chair's back and, as the chair fell away under her, got just the push she needed. Pam North was through the trap to her waist. After that it was still not easy, but she made it.

She lay in a low passage under the roof – a passage too small to be called an attic, a passage empty except for electric conduits. But at the far end, there was a light. She wriggled to it, again bruisingly, on her belly.

The light came from a little window, hinged at the top, fastened at the bottom merely with a latch. She pulled the dusty window open and, only a few feet below it, a roof sloped down gradually. Pam North wriggled through the window, head first since she had no room to turn, caught herself just in time, and came down – shaking – with her feet on the roof. She sat down on it, then, and inched down cautiously.

At its lowest point, the roof was a few feet above another, also sloping down. Pam lowered herself to the new roof, and continued. She moved cautiously, making as little sound as possible. She was, apparently, at the rear of the house. When the man returned – if he had really gone, which had to be chanced – it would be, she hoped, in the station wagon and along the drive. She reached the bottom of the new roof, which was apparently that of a porch, and was only about ten feet from the ground. She hung from the edge, hoped for softness below, and let herself drop.

Landing, she staggered backward and sat down hard. But she sat down in soft earth. She was up again almost at once, and almost at once was running. She caught herself just before she ran into, fell into, a newly dug hole. It was a large hole – large enough to be a grave. Pam skirted it, and ran down a hill, through an open meadow. Now the night was too bright with the little moon – too bright by far. She ran expecting, with each step, a blow in the back. She ran, not looking around at the dim house she had left behind.

She came to a barbed wire fence and crawled under it. A barb caught her already ruined dress — where was her coat? Surely she had had a coat! — and the dress gave. The point of the barb raked, like a harsh fingernail, on Pam's skin. She got up beyond the fence and went on down the hill, now among blueberry bushes and — yes — wild blackberry. Thorns grabbed at her, whipped at her. They lashed her legs. She kept on going.

She went over a stone fence, clutching — she feared — ugly columns of poison ivy. If I live through this, I'll be a mess for days, Pam North said, and stumbled on a hummock. She grabbed wildly, held a sapling briefly, plunged with both feet into water and almost fell. She was, she realized, in a swamp.

It had been then that her mind, which before had been clear enough, if understandably full of fears, began to scream. It had been then the nightmare started. Injustice such as this, Pam's screaming mind insisted, was possible only in a nightmare. If you were fleeing for your life you deserved, at the very least, to flee in dignity. To begin flight with what amounted to a prat-fall, to snag oneself — just where one inevitably does — in going under a barbed wire fence, to be whipped by spiked bushes, now to fall into a swamp, probably full of unpleasant snakes — these things carried life's irony to the point of burlesque. It was as if, facing a firing squad as bravely as possible, one were suddenly to fall uncontrollably to sneezing.

She got hold of herself and began, in the dim light, to work her way to the left. She stumbled often, stepped several times more into cold water, once wrenched her ankle. She made many false turns, false steps, before she came again to firm ground. She then returned, or hoped she did, to her original course, away from the house. She had supposed that soon she would find a road.

She could only guess, on the hilltop, starting down it, with no road yet in evidence, how long it had been since she left the house through the trap door and the little window. She thought it had been several hours and that now it was long after midnight. She was unbearably tired; her body ached. And she had still not found water she dared stop to drink. She came out of the woods and to a mowed field, and on the comparatively level surface Pam North staggered as she walked. Once she fell, catching herself without injury. She did not immediately get up again, but lay as she had fallen on the grass. But she began to feel cold, and managed to get back to her feet.

She went under another barbed wire fence and beyond it came to a brook. It was not a wide brook; there were stones in it on which one could step. Pam lay down on the bank and drank from her cupped hands. No doubt cows drank there; in all likelihood cows waded there. It did not matter. The water was cold in her throat, cold on her face. She got up after a time and, absurdly, wanted a cigarette as she could not remember ever having wanted one. The spirit should flee death, if it must, along a beam of light, Pam thought, being, by then, light-headed. The body is ridiculous.

She crossed the brook, climbed wearily over another stone wall, and stepped down into a lane. Without any hesitation, or any thought, Pam turned to her right and followed the little lane. Inevitably, it climbed a hill. Pam put one foot grimly in front of another.

At the top of the hill, the lane pitched down. A hundred feet down the slope, on her left, there was a small house. Pam walked to the gap in the wall in front of the house and turned and walked up to the house, putting one foot in front of the other. She did not look to either side. She reached the door of the house and knocked, and knocked again.

After a time there was sound from within the house, and then lights went on. The door opened.

A tall man in his thirties stood at the door, and tightened a robe around him. He was blond; he had a long, narrow face and a wide thin mouth, which now widely expressed surprise.

"Well," he said, "hello." He looked at her again. "Hello, hello," he said. "What —"

"My name is North," Pam said. "Pamela North." She was conscious that she mumbled.

"Come again?" the man with the thin face said.

Pam said, "I'm lost – I –"

"You do look it," he said. He opened the door. "Motor smash? Come in and –" He stopped.

Pam had raised both hands, palms outward. She was backing away.

"Hold it," he said. "Come in here and –" Pam was backing away. "I'm perfectly respectable," he said. "Wait. My name's Lyster. Perfectly respectable bloke, for a journalist. You –"

Pam turned.

"I say!" Alec Lyster called after Pam North as she ran from the house, from a man who pronounced "again" to rhyme with "pain," who might be –

She ran past a station wagon parked to one side of the drive. She reached the lane and turned left, and ran along it, stumbling.

Alec Lyster stood for a moment looking after her. Then he walked, taking long strides, to the station wagon.

The sound was loud in the still night as the motor caught. Hearing it, Pam North left the lane and went over a stone wall. She lay behind it, in deep grass.

But *was* it? Pam thought. *Was* it the same voice?

Bill Weigand was explanatory; he was logical; he was patient. Jerry North listened, dully.

There was nothing to suggest that Pam had been in this rambling house at any time. There were, indeed, indications that she had not. Hilda Godwin had been dead for several days; almost certainly she had been dead before Monday night, when Pam had gone to the office of North Books, Inc., with the recording she had — again this was almost, but only almost, certain — received in the mail. It was after that that she had been in the coal bin of the little house on Elm Lane and had left a handkerchief there, by accident or by design. There was evidence that a trunk, probably the trunk from which the swollen body of Hilda Godwin had now been removed, had also been in the basement of the Elm Lane house.

But there was nothing to indicate that the trunk had not been removed from the basement and taken to the country long before Pam had been locked in the coal bin. If one had to guess, one would guess that it had been; that trunk and body had been in the country house since, perhaps, Sunday. Assuming Hilda had been killed in New York – and that was only hypothesis – and brought to the country for burial, there would have been no reason to delay the transportation.

"There may have been," Jerry said. "We don't know what reasons he may have had."

Bill agreed to that. He had said it was a guess. He was only saying he thought it the most probable guess. He was saying only that, so far as they knew, Pam had been last in New York. He was only saying there was nothing to indicate she had been at any time in this rambling house.

They were in a room – a small room, book-filled – off the square central hall. The whole house was lighted; the whole house was full of State policemen. Mullins was with them; they were looking everywhere, for anything.

"I have to get back," Bill Weigand said. "We've got to get things going there. I think you should come with me."

"I think she was here," Jerry said. "I know what you have to do – what your job is."

"If I thought –" Bill began.

"I know," Jerry said. "All the same, you've got your job." He moved a hand out, slowly. "This," he said. "Hilda Godwin murdered and crammed into a trunk. But I've got to find Pam. I –"

But Mullins was standing in the doorway.

Jerry and Bill looked at him.

"There's a room upstairs," Mullins said. "Locked up, and no key. The boys are —"

There was a sound of impact from above, of rending wood.

"— breaking it down," Mullins said. "It looks like maybe —"

Jerry was brushing past Mullins, by then, and Bill Weigand was after him. Mullins followed Weigand.

"— somebody's been locked up in there," Mullins said, and followed the others up the stairs.

It was not immediately apparent whether anyone had been locked in the small room on the second floor. The window was open, and that, since the house would normally have been closed between visits to it by Hilda Godwin, was suggestive. It was several minutes before they found the opening in the ceiling of the closet, and found that a current of cool air came down through it. They found the attic space quickly, then, and the open window at the end of it. By that time, Mullins, working with a trooper, had found prints.

Pam North had been there. At a guess, she had been there recently. She was not there then.

When they were outside the house, throwing the beams of strong lights against it, picking

125

out the little window near the roof, it was not hard to guess which way she had gone. The roof of the house sloped gradually, ended a few feet above the back porch roof which sloped at the same angle. They examined the ground, then.

A woman had dropped from the porch roof; her narrow, sharp-heeled shoes had dug deeply into soft earth. She had staggered backward, off balance, and sat down hard in soft earth, leaving an impression neatly round.

"Pam!" Jerry North said, with conviction.

She had got to her feet again. She had almost fallen into the wide, shallow excavation in the middle of a cleared garden plot. She had gone around it, and she had been running – running away from the house, down a slope. Beyond the cleared square of the garden she had left no tracks they could find in the darkness, even with the best of flashlights.

Jerry could not stop. He ran down the slope, the beam from his flashlight leaping ahead of him.

"Go with him, Mullins," Bill Weigand said. Mullins went.

Three strands of barbed wire made a fence at the bottom of the slope. The beams from two flashlights moved along the fence; it was that from Jerry's which stopped on a small piece of cloth which dangled from a barb on the fence's lowest strand.

It was wool; it was beige wool. Jerry was almost certain. He and Mullins went under the fence.

Beyond it they picked up again, briefly, the signs of someone's passage through tall grass, among bushes. They found, in an area bare of grass, one footprint. They went on to a stone fence, covered luxuriantly with heavy vine. Here and there the vine still carried the bright red leaves which ivy flaunts in autumn.

"That's poison ivy, huh?" Mullins asked. "Seems to me —"

But Jerry North was already going over the wall, through the ivy.

"Jeeze!" Mullins said. Mullins followed Gerald North. He followed him into the swamp beyond the wall.

Bill Weigand watched them go, saw them stop at the bottom of the first slope and examine something; saw them wriggling under the barbed wire fence. He went back into the house, and conferred with the sergeant; then with a physician from the Medical Examiner's office.

At a guess, Hilda Godwin had been killed Saturday night or Sunday. She had, almost certainly, been strangled. It was probable that the body had been put into the trunk within a short time after death. They would see what else they could find out, using knives and chemical reagents. So —

"She was a poet," Bill said, abstractedly. "She wrote love lyrics, I'm told."

"Well," said the physician, without emphasis.

There was nothing more to do in the rambling house beyond South Salem, in upper Westchester — nothing more for an acting captain, Homicide West. There was much to do in town, now that they knew. There was the little house in Elm Lane to be taken apart for what might be hidden in it; there was the past to dig into. And some time, if possible, there was sleep to be got.

"When Mullins gets back —" Acting Captain Weigand began to the State Police sergeant. But he stopped.

A tall, handsome man in his middle forties stood in the doorway and looked at them, his regular features grave, his eyebrows faintly lifted.

"Oh," he said. "Captain Weigand. Something's happened?"

"Yes," Bill Weigand said. "Miss Godwin's dead, Mr. Wilson."

The rather full, well-shaped lips of Professor Bernard Wilson parted; the well-shaped head shook slowly from side to side.

"Dead," Wilson said. "That is shocking, Captain. She was so young. So alive. Dead."

His voice grew heavier as he spoke. It was as if realization came only slowly into his mind, and the shock of realization.

"She did not die naturally?" Wilson said, and there was no real question in his voice.

"No," Bill said. "She was strangled, Mr. Wilson. Several days ago. Her body was there."

He gestured toward the trunk, which stood where they had found it; stood open, but now empty.

Wilson looked at the trunk, and there was an expression of horror on his face.

"Several days," he said. "In —" he nodded toward the trunk.

"Yes," Bill Weigand said.

"How horrible," Wilson said. "How very horrible it must have been."

"Yes," Bill said again. "It always is."

"She was so beautiful," Wilson said. "Really beautiful."

"There's no use thinking about it," Bill said. He waited. He waited pointedly.

"I live near by," Wilson said. "That is, I have a cottage along the road. I use it mostly in the summer, of course. But I happened to be there tonight."

"Did you?" Bill said.

"Yes," Wilson said. "I was working. It is a good place to work, especially at this time of year. I am doing a critical —" He stopped.

"You don't care about that," he said. "I saw the lights — something woke me and I saw the lights. I suppose I heard sirens?"

"Probably," Bill said.

"They must have wakened me," Wilson said. "When I saw the lights I realized something was wrong. I came down the road and saw the police cars."

His voice was fully under control, by then. The uncertainty which shock brings was no longer in it.

"Of course," Wilson said, "I realize there is nothing I can do. I thought there might be."

"When did you come up?" Bill asked him. "Did you see anything? Hear anything?"

Wilson hesitated. He said that he realized, now, that he had seen something. If something had happened that night? He was told something had.

Then, Wilson told Bill Weigand, speaking slowly and carefully, in the modulated voice of his profession, with the careful word choice of his profession, it was possible he could help. What he knew meant nothing to him; it might help others, better trained in evaluating evidence.

"Right," Bill said. "Go on, Mr. Wilson."

Wilson went on. He started with the drink he had had at the Four Corners, where Weigand had seen him, and they had talked with Shaw,

130

with Alec Lyster. As he left the restaurant, Bernard Wilson had planned merely to go to his apartment uptown and read for a time before going to bed. But, as he walked toward the subway, he had had an idea. Or, more exactly perhaps, something he wished to say had suddenly come clear in his mind.

"I'm writing a —" Wilson said, and did not end the sentence immediately, except with a shrug. "Call it a critical history," he said. "I've been working up here all summer, coming up this fall whenever I had the time free. Most of my material is here." When he said "here" he waved generally to his left, presumably indicating his house.

Having tomorrow free — he hesitated, corrected himself — having today free, Wednesday free, he decided to spend the evening in the country and get on with it. He had, therefore, picked up his car and driven to South Salem. He had arrived at about half past eight and had got to work. Oh yes — he had stopped for a sandwich on the way. He worked by a window from which he could look out and down at Hilda Godwin's house. "The old Somerville place, they call it," he said.

Bill merely nodded to that.

He had, he thought, been working less than an hour when he saw the lights of a car approach the Godwin house. The car drove up

131

to the front of the house and stood there, for a time, with the lights on. He saw someone moving, once passing between him and the lights but for the most part keeping on the other side.

"I supposed, of course, that Hilda had arrived," Wilson said. "That is, I supposed she had been here for several days and had been out to dinner somewhere and was coming home."

"Right," Bill said. "Go on."

The lights had gone on in the house, and after a time the lights of the car had been switched off. Wilson had gone back to work; he had thought, vaguely, that if the lights were still on when he finished for the evening, he might walk down and say "hello" to Hilda Godwin.

But after about an hour, or perhaps three-quarters of an hour, the lights went off in the Godwin house, the lights of the car went on, the car backed and turned and left. Hilda, he decided, had stopped by for something, had got it, had gone again.

That was all; he realized it was not much. He had gone back to work; about midnight he had gone to bed. The sirens, he supposed, had wakened him. He had looked out and seen the lights, guessed something was wrong, come to do anything he could.

"I thought she might have been taken ill," he

said. "That the siren was that of an ambulance. I did feel I might help."

Possibly he had, Bill told him. The car had arrived at the house at, was this right, about a quarter after nine? Had gone again at ten or a little after? Bernard Wilson thought so. It took, not hurrying, a couple of hours to drive between this area beyond South Salem and New York?

"Less, if one is in a hurry," Wilson said. "Shaw does it in an hour and a half, he says. When traffic's light, of course."

"Shaw?" Bill Weigand repeated. "He lives near here?"

The Shaws had a summer place in the neighborhood, Wilson said. They seldom visited it after Labor Day. And Alec Lyster had a cabin near by.

"Not much more than a shack," Wilson said. "But comfortable enough. On Farm Road."

"And Mr. Rogers?" Bill asked. "Does he live around here too?"

Not Rogers, Wilson said. He smiled.

"Of course," he said, "this isn't coincidental. It seldom is, is it? Hilda found this house four or five years ago and fell in love with it, and with the country. She kept urging her friends to get places here. The Shaws did – bought a place. Then I rented one. Then Lyster did. One has a tendency to go where one already has friends, you know."

Bill nodded, abstractedly.

"You don't happen to know whether the Shaws came up this evening?" he asked. "Or whether Lyster did?"

Wilson did not. He would be inclined to think they had not. On the other hand, it had been a pleasant evening.

"A pleasant evening," he repeated. "She loved such evenings, Captain. She had such − such awareness." Wilson shook his head. "Such vitality," he said. "To think −" He shook his head again. "I met her first when she was almost a child, you know," he said. "She was in one of my classes. It was as if − as if there were a light in the class."

There was nothing to say. Bill said nothing.

"It was in her poetry," Wilson said. "It would have been in her novels."

"Speaking of the novel," Bill said, "did you know the manuscript has been − misplaced?"

Wilson emerged from nostalgia. He raised expressive eyebrows; he shook his head.

"After you returned it," Bill said. "At least, that's what I understand from Mr. Rogers. It seems to have disappeared from the receptionist's desk."

"Disappeared?" Wilson repeated. "That's very strange. Do you mean someone misappropriated it? Does Rogers think that?"

Bill shrugged. He said that apparently no one knew what to think. The manuscript had vanished.

"They've misplaced it," Wilson said. "It's a large firm, you know. All very carefully organized. The sort of place in which all sorts of things disappear for days."

It could be that, Bill agreed. No doubt it was. But so far the manuscript had been traced only to the receptionist's desk.

"Is it important?" Wilson asked. "There'll be copies, of course. There always are. No doubt her agent has at least one."

Bill supposed so. They had not yet come across a copy. Mr. Rogers had looked for a copy. But no doubt Wilson was right.

"Of course," Wilson said. "A copy will turn up, unquestionably." He paused. "You don't feel it has anything to do with this?" he asked, and nodded, uncomfortably, at the trunk.

It was difficult to see what the connection could be, Bill agreed. Nevertheless, it was strange, out of the ordinary. When things out of the ordinary, however trivial in themselves, turned up in relation, however distant, to murder, one — well, thought twice.

Wilson shook his head.

"I read it," he said. "You won't find anything in it to help you, I'm quite sure. An autobiographical novel by a young woman — by a

135

young woman who happened to have great talent, who often hit on miraculous phrases. But still, nothing too far out of the ordinary. Her second novel might have been that. This was interesting, showed her special flair, but remained innocuous. She used her own life, people she had known, as first novelists almost always do."

"People she had known?" Bill said.

"Of course," Professor Bernard Wilson told him. "Who else? But very tenderly, Captain. Very appreciatively. I can see myself in it, to be sure — myself and others she knew. That is inevitable. She was rather perceptive about us, Captain. But gentle. Almost tender, it seemed to me. She was like that, you know."

"Was she?" Bill said. "I didn't know, of course. It isn't often the gentle people who are murdered, of course."

This time it had been, Wilson assured him. This time it most certainly had been.

"By the way," Bill asked, "what did she call the book?"

"Oh," Wilson said, "she called it 'Come Up Smiling.' Not a very good title, I'm afraid. Probably it will have to be changed."

"If they find it," Bill said.

"I've no doubt they'll find it," Wilson said. He waited. "Well?" he said. "Can I do anything?"

Bill Weigand was afraid he could do no more than he had done. It was quite probable he had helped.

VII

Wednesday, 3:10 A.M. to 5:30 A.M.

Pam North lay behind the stone wall, in wet grass, cold dampness spreading through her. She shivered; nervousness and cold combined to make her teeth chatter. She was absurdly afraid, as she heard the station wagon coming down the road toward her, that the chattering of her teeth would reveal her. She set her teeth hard together.

The car, invisible from where she lay (as she prayed she would be invisible to its occupant), passed slowly down the road. She could see the lights, which briefly made the pale night white. The car passed, and she did not move. She heard it continue, still slowly, down the road. She waited. After a few minutes, the sound of its motor died away, but she still did not move. After several more minutes, she got to her knees and then, crouching, to her feet.

She saw headlights and dropped back to concealment in the wet grass. She heard the motor again, as the car approached, again

138

the lights whitened the top of the wall, leaving her in a trough of darkness. The car still moved slowly, and again it passed. She was certain it was the station wagon she had seen in the yard of the man – what was his name? – whose intonation and pronunciation were British. She was certain that, in it, the man was looking for her.

Was his the voice? Pam North thought again, and found she could not be sure. She did not know, now, whether she would ever be sure. If she could not, this strange nightmare of flight was without purpose. She heard the car move back along the narrow road and then, while its sound was still clear in the night, the motor stopped. After a moment, straining her ears, she heard another sound which might be that of a door closing. Still for some moments she lay quiet, the damp cold biting into her.

When finally she roused herself, she got to her feet and began to walk, gropingly, inside the wall, parallel to the road, away from the house to which, she was almost certain, the man had returned. She continued to the length of one field, but then came to a closely articulated wire fence. Pam North went back over the wall, then, and down the road. She was too tired to run and could not see her way to run. As she walked, she kept looking back over her shoulder.

How long she went, furtive, through the semi-darkness, along the narrow road, she did not know and could afterward hardly estimate. She lost track of time; she lost any real consciousness of movement, except that each forward step came to be an ordeal almost beyond endurance. She did not pass any more houses or, if she did, they were set too far back from the road to be visible. She had begun by running for safety; now she crept. The light weight wool of the dress, damp now, the dress shapeless, clung to her body. It was blotched with coal dust and with mud; there was coal dust in Pam's hair and streaked on her face.

As she walked, Pam suddenly became conscious that she was sobbing like a child, and that she could not stop this.

She went on, one foot in front of the other, on the winding little road. It climbed and descended; vaguely, she felt that, in total, it bent to her right. But that meant nothing. The only thing that meant anything was that sometime, somewhere, this back road must come to another, more frequented road, and that that road would reach another; that sometime she would reach the help of other people and then, perhaps, find Jerry again. But no – Jerry was in California. Jerry knew nothing of this.

She had no idea, now, where she was in relation to the house from which she had fled. She might, indeed, be circling back toward it. She realized this, but the realization was dim – the possibility seemed without importance. She would take this step, and then this step, and where the steps took her she could not control.

She was walking on the right of the road, finding the way with her feet more than with her eyes. She walked into the station wagon before she saw it. Her hands came up to protect her face and body and touched the hood of the wagon. She leaned against it, for a moment, glad of the support. But then, as if she had in fact been walking in her sleep, she awakened.

She did not recognize the station wagon. Even in daylight, she realized, she would not be able to tell, finally, whether this station wagon – or any other – was the one into which she had been pushed, tied up, in a fenced-in yard somewhere in the city. But, by now, any station wagon was inimical. When she realized what she was leaning against, Pam North recoiled. She pushed herself away, as if she were pushing away the vehicle itself.

She staggered with weariness as she rejected support, and almost fell. She recovered and started toward the nearest wall. But as she reached it, she stopped. Looking, as she could after she had moved, through the station wagon she realized that it was unoccupied. It had been parked on the narrow shoulder, jutting somewhat into the road. There was, so far as she could see, no house near by, and no driveway leading to a house. A station wagon – a big one, she thought a new one – had merely been pulled to the wrong side of a back road deep in the country and left there.

She waited briefly and listened anxiously. She heard no sound, except the movement of the wind through trees. Cautiously, she re-approached the station wagon. She looked into the darkness in all directions; then she tried the left hand door. It would open only part way before it hit bushes along the road, but it opened far enough. Pam climbed into the station wagon.

Of course, it would be locked. Even in deep country, no one left a valuable station wagon by the roadside with the ignition unlocked. She slid behind the wheel; reached, without thought, for the ignition switch.

There was, as she had expected, no key in the switch. It was, as she had known –

Her fingers pressed on the switch. It turned. The key had been taken, but the car had nevertheless been left unlocked.

She turned the switch off again, and looked into the rear of the wagon. Something was lying on the floor there, behind the second seat. Pam leaned back, far back. When that failed, she climbed back – slowly, shakingly.

Her hands closed on the wool of a blanket. She moved it. Under the wadded blanket there was a coat — a woman's coat. Pamela North's coat.

This, then, was the station wagon! Not the one the man who had stood at the door of a cottage, and pronounced "again" to rhyme with "pain" had driven after her. Because that one, surely —

Pam shook her head. Nothing was sure. It had been a long time since she had heard, as she thought, that other station wagon return to the yard of the cottage. During that time, the man might have driven anywhere; he could easily have circled, knowing back roads, and come to this place long before she could walk to it and then — But her mind gave it up. Why would he abandon the station wagon in a place where she would almost certainly find it, if she lasted long enough? There was no answer.

There was, however, an immediate need. That was to get away. Pam, moving as rapidly as her weary, and somewhat battered, body could be moved, got back behind the wheel. She turned the ignition switch again, and then she stepped on the accelerator. That was how their own car was started.

It was how this one was started. There was a heavy sigh under the hood, as the cold motor turned. There was a whir, then, and the motor caught. Pam reached for the light switch on the panel and found it, and the lights went on.

She could not go in the direction the car faced; she had come from that direction, and there there was only danger. Laboriously, wrenching at the wheel, Pam cut and backed, cut and went forward, cut and backed again. Once one rear wheel sank alarmingly into something and, when she started forward again, that wheel spun for a moment. Then it caught.

She made it on that turn, which was lucky, since it would have been risky to back again. She straightened the car on the narrow road and drove, not rapidly, certainly with no confidence, toward whatever lay ahead.

She drove a Buick station wagon which carried New York license plates numbered HG-7425. This was an unusual number for New York, it indicated that the owner of the car had gone to some slight trouble to express individuality.

They had found nothing further to prove, nothing even to indicate, that they were following a path Pam had followed before them. Mullins pointed this out; Mullins was patient. His voice, not normally gentle, was gentle now.

"Look," Mullins said. "I know how you feel, Mr. North. We all do. We'll find her. But this don't get us anywhere. How do we know she

144

didn't go that way?" He gestured. "Or that way?" He waited.

Jerry merely called his wife's name in the quiet night. He called and kept on going. He did not hurry, now, as he had hurried, without rest, without sleep, for more than twenty hours. He merely walked on through fields, calling, "Pam! *Pam!*" and hearing no answer.

It took them less time than it had taken Pam to find a way around the swamp. They went on, Jerry leading, with each step farther from the house. That was the answer, although Jerry did not make it to Mullins. Fleeing, Pam would flee away, along as direct a course as she could manage. It was all they had to go on.

They crossed a brook on stepping stones, and if they had been a dozen feet to the left, they might have seen the depressed grass where she had lain to drink, to cup water onto her face. But they missed this. They came to a wall and went over it, through poison ivy again, and came to a narrow lane. They stopped there. The problem was too obvious to need words. But then Jerry started along the road to his right. It was not, he thought, quite the toss of a coin. Given the need to turn one way or the other, with no special incentive to choice, most right-handed people turn toward the right. Jerry had himself turned so, before he rationalized his choice.

They climbed a hill and, beyond it, saw a cabin near the road.

"May as well ask," Mullins said, and they turned into a drive, passed a station wagon parked on roughly cut grass, knocked on a door. After a time a tall young man appeared at the door, tightening a robe around his waist.

"Now what have we?" he enquired. His tone was one of exasperated patience.

They told him. Halfway through, he began to nod his head.

"She was here," he said. "Very bedraggled, if I may say so. Rather dirty, you know, as if she'd been in a dust bin. I said, 'What now, lady?' or words to that effect, and she took off. Can't imagine why."

"Which way?" Jerry asked.

It was no good, he told them. He'd had a try at it. She'd gone up the road, running. She'd worried him. He'd taken the car — "Silly thing to do, come to think of it" — and gone after her. He'd gone up the road a mile or more, slowly, found nobody, come back. He'd decided she must have had a car herself, up the road, although he had not heard it start nor seen anything of it.

"What's the row?" he asked.

Mullins told him that, or enough of it. There had been trouble at Miss Godwin's house; Mrs. North had found it necessary —

146

"Trouble?" the man at the door asked. "What kind of trouble?"

Mullins hesitated. Then he said, "Murder."

"Not Hilda?" the man said, quickly. "Hilda's all right?" Mullins regarded him. "She's a friend of mine," the man said. "A good friend."

"She's not all right," Mullins said. "She's dead, Mr. —?"

"Lyster," the man said. "Alec Lyster. Good God! Who — ? This gal you're trying to find?"

"Not Mrs. North," Mullins said. Jerry North had left them; he was walking toward the road. He stopped and looked at the station wagon and then crossed and looked into it. "Wait a minute, Mr. North," Mullins said. Jerry stopped, his hands on the side of the station wagon.

Mullins said, "It wasn't Mrs. North killed her. It wasn't any woman. You're a friend of hers, you say?"

Lyster said, "Yes."

"Could be the Loot'ud like to talk to you," Mullins said. "I mean the Captain."

"Listen," Lyster said. "You're sure Hilda —?"

"That's right," Mullins said. "She is. I'm a police detective, Mr. Lyster. I'd like you to come along and talk to the Captain, if you don't mind. We'll look for Mrs. North on the way."

Lyster hesitated. Then he nodded; said, "Wait till I dress, will you, old man?" and went into the cabin at Mullins's acquiescing nod.

Jerry left the station wagon; he walked to the road; he turned left and began to walk along the road. Mullins made no effort to stop him.

Lyster was quick. When he came out, he looked enquiringly at Mullins, made a gesture with his head toward the place Jerry North had stood.

"The lady who was here's his wife," Mullins said. "We better take your car."

They took the station wagon. A hundred yards up the road they stopped for Jerry North. He got in, saying nothing. They drove on slowly. After a time Mullins, who was watching to their right, the beam from his flashlight moving on the road's shoulder, said "Hold it!" Lyster stopped the car and Mullins got out. He examined the shoulder; he crossed and examined that on the other side. He got back in.

"Was a car here," he told them. "Parked facing that way." He jerked a thumb. "Turned around. Went in the ditch a little and pulled out. Went the way we're going."

"I said she might have a car," Lyster told them.

"She didn't," Mullins said. "But —"

"Someone had," Jerry said. He swore, in a hopeless voice.

It was not far by road to the house Hilda Godwin had summered in and Alec Lyster clearly knew the way. Bill Weigand came out when he heard the car; he looked at Jerry, who shook his head slowly; at Mullins, who lifted heavy shoulders. "Looks like she's in a car," Mullins said. He said, "This is Mr. Lyster. He was a friend of Miss Godwin. Thought you might like —"

"Right," Bill said. He put a hand on Jerry North's shoulder. "We'll find her," he said.

"Sure," Jerry said, his voice dull. "Sure."

"Oh," Lyster said, "so it's you, Captain."

"Yes," Bill said. "I heard you lived near by. You've heard what's happened."

Lyster nodded.

"Do you know anything about it?" Bill asked.

"Good God, no!"

"Did you hear anything tonight? See anything. You came here after you left the restaurant?"

Lyster had not, he said, seen or heard anything. He had left the Shaws at the restaurant; he had taken Miss Barclay to the theater at which she was playing. He had been at loose ends; the night had been fine and he had decided to spend it in the country. He had been asleep when Pam had wakened him, and fled from him — "rather a shock, that" — and had got to sleep again to be once more awakened, this time by Jerry North and Mullins, and "this dismal business about poor Hilda."

149

"Who'd do this to her?" he asked.

"I don't know, yet," Bill said. "We'll find out, Mr. Lyster. You're staying on in the country?"

Lyster shook his head. He would, he said, drive back to the city. "O.K.?"

He was told it was. He gave his city address. He nodded when Bill said they'd probably drop around to talk to him later.

"Is she —?" Lyster asked. He nodded toward the house.

"No," Bill Weigand said. "She isn't, Mr. Lyster. In any case —" He let the inflection of his voice finish the sentence. Lyster's voice shook a little when he said, "D'y mind telling me — how?"

"Strangled," Bill said. "Her body put in a trunk. Several days ago, Mr. Lyster."

Lyster swore, his voice low. He went to the station wagon without saying anything more and backed it into the road, and drove it down the road.

"Hit him hard," Mullins said. "Didn't it?"

"Apparently," Bill said. "It's not a pretty idea, Sergeant. Come on, Jerry."

Jerry North looked at him.

"Pam may be in town by now," Bill told him. "Anyway, there's nothing we can do here. The State boys have got a report out on her. They'll — search around here."

He waited.

"All right," Jerry said. "I don't know what to do. Whatever you say."

They drove back to town. As they drove, Bill talked, and was silent, and talked again. Although he knew that Weigand was talking more to himself than to anyone, Mullins listened, now and then put in a word of agreement. Jerry North did not speak; he only half listened. He pushed the car's speed higher with his mind; although Mullins drove fast enough.

She's all right, Jerry thought. *She's got a car and driven home. She'll be in the apartment, waiting. She'll —*

He had sent a man up to the Wilson house, Bill told them both, and was heard by Mullins. As a check, solely — to make certain that Professor Wilson could see from there what he said he had seen. He could have. He was not, however, there. Evidently he, too, had returned to town.

"Why?" Mullins asked.

"I don't know, Sergeant," Bill told him.

"We haven't got much, and that's a fact," Mullins said, turning west on New York 35.

"A dead burglar," Bill said. "A dead poet. A missing record. A missing book manuscript. Four men."

One of the men had loved the girl and planned to marry her. According to him, another of the men, although already married,

151

had loved her too, and refused rejection. A third, Wilson, had known her years before; had found that she was a light in a university classroom. To the fourth she was a friend, but his voice shook when he thought of her dead.

"Anybody might," Mullins pointed out. "Like you said, the idea ain't pretty."

He turned left on Route 21, followed it past the entrance to the Pound Ridge Reservation, slowed for sharp curves and increased speed again.

"Of course," Bill Weigand said, "it doesn't have to be any of these people."

Mullins sighed deeply at that. He yawned widely. He said that, anyway, it had to be a man. He was told that he was jumping to conclusions.

"Some women have strong hands," Bill Weigand said. "I should think, for example, that a woman sculptor might have."

Mullins did not take his eyes from the road. It was nevertheless as if he looked at Weigand with surprise.

"It's early days," Weigand said, and yawned himself. "And a long day."

They left Jerry North at the door of his apartment house. He was, Bill told him, to try to get some sleep. Nobody, Bill told him, could go on forever without sleep.

Jerry said, "Sure," in a dull voice, but as he

152

went into the building he began to hurry. When the elevator did not come quickly, he went up the stairs, and as he climbed he was almost running. He was breathless in front of the door to the apartment; he fumbled for his keys. He called, *"Pam!"* as he was opening the door.

The apartment was as he had left it. His bags stood where he had left them. Three cats sat and looked at Jerry North, their eyes round with wonder, with expectancy.

Jerry crouched suddenly and picked up the nearest cat; he held her at arm's length.

"Where is she?" he demanded.

The blue eyes were flat and inscrutable. The cat wriggled. Jerry put her down.

He went through the empty apartment, not calling any longer. Then he returned and sat in a chair in the living room, near the telephone. He started to light a cigarette, but when he had taken one from a package he merely held it, unlighted and forgotten, between his fingers.

There were no road signs on the back roads, and one narrow twisting road led only to another, no wider, no more traveled or better surfaced. It seemed that, steering the heavy station wagon, she might wander forever through night along roads which led nowhere. She was almost unbearably tired, now; her eyes ached, her body ached. She had no idea how long she had been driving the car, which seemed sluggish, which drifted sullenly to the right on the crowned roads. She came to a Y, unmarked: two roads, neither promising anything, continued diagonally, anonymously, to left and right.

Pam stopped the car. She put her arms on the wheel and her head on her arms. It's no good, she thought. There'll never be an end.

She sat so for minutes. She raised her head, shifted her hands to the rim of the wheel, started the car moving down the road which angled to the right. One way was as good as another; all were meaningless.

Probably there were darkened houses on either side and people slept in the houses. The road led somewhere. But she could not see the houses. She could see only the road, lighted by the spreading beams of the headlights. She could only drive on, slowly, groping through the night.

She drove a little more than a mile from the Y. Then a word leaped at her: "Stop." For a moment, it seemed to her that the word existed only in her mind. But then she brought the car to a stop and read, above and below the reflected command, the words: "Thru Traffic." And here there was a road sign. She could see it only dimly, could not make out the words. She pressed a button on the floor of the car with a toe and the lights lifted.

"New York 57 mi." the sign told her, and pointed to the left. She turned onto a deserted road, and the wheels steadied on concrete. She drove toward New York, the lights slicing the darkness. As she drove, she went faster and faster. Her hands tightened on the wheel.

She tried to think clearly what was happening, but she still thought as one thinks in a dream. Ideas slipped away, distorted themselves in her mind. She had to get it and take it to the police, to Bill, and then she would be safe, she thought, but she could not, at first, remember what it was that had to be taken to the police. Then she remembered – the record. But then she thought, no, I must find it and break it and then I can tell him –

It was not clear. The big car went faster and faster through the night.

The lights picked up signs, held them for an instant, relinquished them. She was on N.Y. 22. She was – "30 M.P.H." a sign said. "Bedford Village," a sign said. A sign said, "School Crossing, Slow." She slowed a little, on the deserted road, in the darkness; went slowly through a sleeping village.

A sign said, "Armonk" and a yellow traffic light blinked on and off, on and off. Beyond it a sign pointed: "White Plains." She turned left, following the arrow of the sign.

Before she reached White Plains there was another sign, and she slowed the station wagon to read it. "New York via Parkways," she read, and turned right down a grade. She knew where she was, then. It was as if light suddenly had been turned on. She found the Bronx River Parkway Extension and drove along it to the Hawthorne Circle. She went three-fourths of the way around the circle, and south on the Saw Mill River Parkway.

She remembered, when she was almost past the last turnoff, that if she stayed on the Parkway she would have to pay toll twice, and that she had no money. I forgot my bag, Pam thought. I left it somewhere. She shook her head a little, trying to remember, and could not. She turned right on the road to Yonkers.

She had not driven through Yonkers for years, but something in her remembered streets. She found Broadway, and went down it, driving more slowly now. There was beginning to be traffic; she had to swing around trucks, slow and even stop at intersections. But she drove still as if in a cage of glass, seeing but cut off from the stirring life around her. The people on the other side of the glass could not help her. Nobody could help her until she had found the record where she had hidden it. There was no safety until she had the record again. Nobody could help her until she had retrieved the record. It was a talisman. It shone in her mind. Nothing else was real in her shaking mind.

She reached and crossed the Broadway bridge over the Harlem and then, after a little, turned right again. Having circumvented the toll booths, she regained the Parkway and went south on it, in a cage of glass. The car became her consciousness; her hands on the wheel, her foot on the accelerator were alive, instinctive. Her mind said only, over and over, I've got to get it before he does, I've got to get it before he does.

The thing to do was to stop for a time. No one can go forever without sleep. There is little to be done at a few minutes after five in the morning, when body and mind are numbed.

Bill Weigand and Mullins sat in Weigand's office. Neither mentioned that it would be a good thing to stop for a time, to sleep for a time. They had been persuasive to that end when they talked to Jerry North. Or perhaps they had; Bill doubted it. It did not apply to them; could not apply until a too impetuous young woman named Pamela North was found again. It was maddening to work as they had to, from the circumference toward the center, working slowly and with care, as if each fact

157

discovered were another brick removed from a collapsed building which had fallen around a woman and imprisoned her.

There was no certainty that, when they got all the bricks removed, they would find her there — that with the solution of the murder they would achieve rescue. It was merely the only way for them to go about it.

The rest — the immediate search for a bright-haired woman of a certain weight, wearing a beige wool dress — was of necessity, and for the moment, in other hands. The description was out; all over the city, in all the area around New York, men were watching. They were watching a man named Garrett Shaw, and looking for a man named Gilbert Rogers. When they reached New York, a professor of creative writing at Dyckman University was to be taken under observation, and a sharp-featured young Englishman named Alec Lyster. License numbers of the cars owned by Wilson and Lyster had been ascertained and written in many notebooks. Mullins himself had passed along the number of Rogers's car.

There was another license number in the notebooks — HG-7425, the number which Hilda Godwin had gone to the trouble to obtain. The car so licensed was a Buick station wagon, on a Roadmaster chassis.

In addition, men from the Mercer Street

station had been taking apart the little house in Elm Lane, seeking any secrets it might hide. So far as the reports showed, it had as yet revealed none.

Bill Weigand rubbed his weary eyes with his finger tips. He read reports – reports hastily got together during the night, of necessity fragmentary, limited to the barest facts; reports on people.

Hilda Godwin would have been twenty-seven in the spring, a report told Bill Weigand. She had been born in New York, and born to money. Her parents had died when she was still a child. She had studied at Dyckman University. When she was nineteen she had begun to publish poetry in magazines; there had been a book of poems when she was twenty-one and another in each of the following years. By the time of the third book, people who had never thought of reading poetry were reading that of Hilda Godwin. Her beauty, which was unquestionable and responded to photography, had helped; her youth had helped; her publishers had helped. Beyond those things, although the report from Sergeant Stein did not specifically so say, there had been some special quality in the poems themselves – there must have been, Bill Weigand thought. He wondered what; some time, he thought, he would try to find out – after other things had been found out.

The poetry had stopped after the third book; it appeared that Hilda Godwin had for a time merely played. Then she had returned to writing, this time prose. She had bought the little house two years before; she had been as often away from it as in it. So —

Weigand laid the report aside. It did not sum up a life, briefly lived, one would guess lived vividly. It left a name and an age, and the titles of three books; it added to the record.

Garrett Shaw came up next; his report was brief. Age, 43. Occupation, art dealer. Married to Alfrieda Shaw, apparently well known as a sculptor. "Modern; reasonably representational," Stein, who had dictated the report, noted. Extent of acquaintance with Hilda Godwin still to be investigated. Whereabouts at critical times still to be determined. "Note: Times of murders not established." Lived on Gramercy Park.

Wilson, Bernard. Age 47. Master of Arts, Doctor of Philosophy; associate professor of English at Dyckman. On Dyckman faculty fifteen years; best known, as teacher, for seminar classes in creative writing. Well known as critic and essayist. Conducted radio symposiums, on Sunday afternoons, on literary subjects; had been, from 1946 to 1948, an editor of *Sweepings*, which had been a poetry magazine. Folded, November, 1948." Educated

Columbia University and Oxford (Rhodes Scholar). Doctorate, Harvard. Extent of association with Hilda Godwin undetermined. "No informants available. Appears possible she may have attended his classes; times coincide."

That was Wilson, from the records. Bill Weigand put the report aside.

Alec Lyster was nearer the age Hilda Godwin had been. He was twenty-eight. He had been in the United States for the past three years; he was an occasional correspondent, mostly by mail, of three British newspapers (listed) and a magazine. He was an occasional contributor to *Punch,* on the American way of life; to the *Atlantic Monthly,* on the British way of life. Wrote some light verse. Lived on the upper West Side, near the drive, in one room apartment. Much in company of Madeleine Barclay, actress. "Bit parts." Extent of relationship with Hilda Godwin undetermined. "Note: Most of this from friend of his found at Four Corners. Informant says saw good deal of H. G. year or so ago."

Rogers, Gilbert. Age, 34. Employed as an editor, Hudson Press. Arrested speeding (Riverside Drive) 1951; altercation with arresting officer; no indication intoxication; fined $25, which paid. Joined staff of Hudson Press in autumn of 1949, coming on from Chicago, where had worked in another publishing house.

Extent of relationship with H.G. undetermined. Whereabouts during presumptive critical periods unknown.

There was a general summary from Stein: "All we can dig up on these people at moment. Sources difficult to contact. No records on anybody but Rogers."

They had, Weigand thought, got a good deal in a few night hours. There was a good deal more left to get. Bill Weigand tapped the fingers of his right hand rhythmically on the desk at which he sat. He could use a break.

The telephone rang. Bill Weigand's voice sounded weary in his own ears as he answered.

"Man named Shaw out here," a voice said. "Says he's got to see you."

"Right," Bill said. "Send him in."

VIII

Wednesday, 5:30 A.M. to 6:08 A.M.

Sergeant Mullins said, "What the hell?" and Bill Weigand, tapping the desk with his fingers, shook his head. Then the door opened with sudden violence, a heavy, dark man filled the doorway, a heavy voice rumbled.

"What's this about Hilda?" Garrett Shaw demanded.

He looked as if he had dressed hastily; his soft shirt was open at the neck, a day's beard was dark on his face. The skin over his right cheekbone was reddened; in the center of the area there was a small cut, the blood dried on it.

Weigand did not hurry his answer. After a moment, he said, "She's dead, Mr. Shaw. She was strangled."

"You talked about a burglar," Shaw told him. "Said she was all right."

"I didn't know, then," Bill told him. "We only found out a few hours ago." He looked up at Shaw. "How did you know?" he asked.

Shaw came into the room. He stood over

Weigand's desk and stared down at Weigand.

"You know a man named Rogers?" he asked. "You know him?"

"Yes," Bill said.

"He just tried to kill me," Shaw said. "He's gone crazy. Did you know that?"

Bill shook his head.

"Comes in yelling," Shaw said. "Jumps me. Yells about Hilda. About — I don't know what. I had to knock him down." He put his hands on the desk. He leaned down toward Bill Weigand. "Tried to kill me," he said, and the heavy rumbling voice filled the little office as a shout would have filled it. "You sit there on —"

"Take it easy, Mr. Shaw," Mullins said, and left his desk near the window. "Just take it easy." Shaw was a big man, but Mullins looked bigger as he came across the office. "Just sit down and take it easy," Mullins said.

Shaw looked at Mullins. He looked at Bill Weigand.

"Right," Bill said. "Sit down, Mr. Shaw. Tell me what you're talking about."

It took shape slowly.

Shaw had been in his apartment, asleep. His wife had gone to Chicago, leaving on the midnight train. He had seen her off, stopped on the way home for a drink, gone to bed about two. He thought it was about an hour ago that the door bell of his apartment had wakened

164

him. Someone had pushed the bell and kept on pushing. Shaw had, sleepily, gone to the door and opened it and Gilbert Rogers had pushed in, and pushed the door closed behind him. He had, at first, merely cursed Garrett Shaw.

"Couldn't make head or tail of it," Shaw told them, leaning toward Bill's desk, putting heavy hands on it. "Incoherent. I tell you, the man's gone crazy."

What had come out after a little, Shaw said, was that Hilda was dead; that somebody had killed her. What had come out was the re- peated, the loudly repeated – "the man was yelling" – assertion that Shaw wouldn't get away with it.

"Wait," Bill said. "He was accusing you of killing Miss Godwin? Is that what it was?"

"You know," Shaw said, "I'm damned if I know. I suppose so. It must have been that. But he didn't say that. He just – yelled. Then he swung at me."

He raised his hand to his damaged cheek. "Landed," he said. "Wears a ring or something. Cut me. See?"

"Yes," Bill said. "Then?"

"Yelling all the time," Shaw said. "About Hilda. About some novel she'd written. What's that got to do with it?"

"I don't know yet," Bill said. "Go on."

"It never made any sense," Shaw said. "Here I

165

was, half asleep at first, and he busts in yelling and swinging. The first time he hit me it staggered me, and then he came at me with his hands out. As if he was going to choke me. I ducked, and tried to make him hear me, and he didn't listen. I said, 'Hold it,' and — oh, I don't know. It was like talking to a crazy drunk." He seemed to think of that. "Maybe he was drunk," he said.

Bill Weigand shook his head. He said he doubted it.

"He had seen Miss Godwin's body," he said. "It may — it was rather shocking, you know. He was going to marry her, I understand."

"Thought he was, maybe," Shaw said. "Her body? Where was this?"

Bill told him. Shaw swore in his rumbling voice. He swore with apparent bitterness. He thumped the desk with a clenched hand.

Weigand waited.

"Were you in love with her, Mr. Shaw?" he asked then.

Shaw looked up.

"Me?" he said.

"Rogers seemed to think you were," Bill told him. "Or had been. That you were — insistent."

"Liar," Shaw said. "Crazy liar. Thought any man who looked at her was —" He broke off.

"You did look at her?" Bill said. Shaw merely

166

stared at him. Bill waited. Then he said, "Well, Mr. Shaw?"

"All right," Shaw said. "Say I did. So what? Listen. I knew about this stuffed —" He stopped. Bill waited again.

But the moment, if there had been a moment, had passed. The violence with which Shaw had entered the office seemed suddenly to flow away. It left a different man — it left a man who leaned back in the chair; who now smiled faintly.

"Very well," he said. "I asked the lady. The lady declined. I said, thank you very much, sorry to have been a trouble."

He was less convincing so.

"Did Rogers, in so many words, accuse you of killing Miss Godwin?"

Shaw shrugged.

"As I told you," he said, "he yelled all sorts of things. Maybe that I'd killed her. Then it sounded as if maybe he'd killed her and was going to kill me. Anyway, he made a stab at killing me. I had to knock him out."

He said this casually. Bill waited.

"Knocked him down, anyway," Shaw said. "He got up and came after me and I knocked him down again. I was — well, I was awake enough by then."

"Yes," Bill said, "I can see you would have been. And —"

"I decided to call you people," Shaw said. "I didn't want to but — hell, he might have had a gun or something."

Shaw had, he said, gone to a telephone in the next room. He had started to dial when he heard movement in the foyer. He had got back just as the door slammed after Rogers. He —

The telephone rang. It was the man who had been keeping an eye on Shaw. He was reporting, unhappily, that he had lost his man. His man had come bursting out of the apartment house and got a cab. It was the only cab in blocks of early morning streets. Where he had gone —

"All right," Bill said. "He came here. He says he had a visitor about an hour ago. You see a visitor?"

He listened. He said, "Right."

He looked up and Shaw was leaning toward him.

"You had a man following me?" Shaw said. His rumbling voice was harsh again.

"I wanted to know what you did," he said. "I want to know what all of you have been doing."

"All of — whom?" Shaw demanded.

"Rogers," Bill said. "One or two others who" — he hesitated momentarily — "were in Miss Godwin's circle," he finished. "Who, for one thing, might have been mentioned in this book she wrote." He waited a moment, looking in-

168

tently at Shaw. "The book that's disappeared," he said. "The book which was, I'm told, autobiographical."

"I don't −" Shaw began. He was calm again. Now he looked a little puzzled. But then he said, "Oh."

"Right," Bill said. "In autobiographical novels, people write about people who have been in their lives, of course. Perhaps Miss Godwin did, Mr. Shaw. Perhaps somebody − didn't like what she wrote."

"That," Shaw told him, "is crazy, Captain."

It could be, Bill agreed. He had, in fact, been told that the book was innocuous. But −

"Who said that?" Shaw demanded.

Bill Weigand told him. Shaw's eyes narrowed momentarily. But then he nodded.

"So?" he said. "Wilson ought to know. It's his field, after all."

Bill Weigand nodded. Professor Wilson ought to know. But he spoke with no apparent assurance, and Shaw waited.

"It's possible," Bill said, "that whatever may have been − resented − was apparent only to the person concerned. Perhaps it revealed a secret of some sort which this person had shared with Miss Godwin; that she revealed in such a way that it wouldn't be a revelation at all to the ordinary reader."

"Then," Shaw said, "what would be the fuss?

I mean —" He shrugged.

Fuss was an odd term for murder, but Bill Weigand did not voice the thought. He merely said he didn't know. He added, "Yet." Shaw waited as if for him to continue. When he did not, Shaw stood up suddenly.

"Well," he said, "that's my story. What do you do about it?"

"Oh," Bill said, "find Mr. Rogers, of course. Ask him what it was all about. You want to make charges against him — assault?"

Shaw hesitated. Then he shook his head.

"The guy's crazy," he said. "He's got enough trouble." Bill nodded. Shaw turned abruptly, and went out the door.

"What d'y know?" Mullins said. "It's a screwy one, all right. You mean that about the book? About some guy who's a character in a book and gets sore and —" Mullins gave it up, shaking his head.

"I don't know, Sergeant," Bill said. "You don't like it?"

"Jeeze," Sergeant Mullins said, and reached for a telephone which began to ring. He said, "O.K.," and wrote a name and telephone number on a pad. He said, "Keep at it, fella," and cradled the telephone.

"Seems you wanted this," he said, and pushed the pad toward Weigand. "Name of the gal's agent. Literary Agent."

"Right," Bill said, and, eyes on the pad, reached for the telephone.

His own voice awoke him. He was crying out something, but the words he used faded with the dream as he came awake. The horror of the dream remained, although the shape of the dream wavered, dissolved in his mind. Pam had been falling and he had stretched out his hands to save her, but as he touched her her body was impalpable between his hands — or was it that his hands were without substance? — and she fell on, screaming. But there was a trunk and it was Pam's body in the trunk, yet as he looked down on it the body changed and was not hers. "She'll be all right," Bill Weigand said. "Don't you worry" and then he was in an airplane, falling in tighter and tighter, ever more dizzying, circles. Pam was with him, falling too, but now there was no airplane and they were falling free in circles, she always beyond his reach. It was there, he thought, groping back, the dream ended. It had ended with someone screaming, and that had wakened him.

He was sitting in a chair in the apartment, his head twisted a little to one side. He called, "Pam?" while he was still only partly awake and from another room a cat began to talk, harshly. Jerry North looked at his watch; the hands pointed to five forty-five. He had not slept long. He remembered, now. He had sat in front of the telephone. For a time one of the cats had sat on his lap. He had told himself the telephone would ring and he would hear Pam's voice, or Bill's, saying that Pam was found. But the telephone had not rung. He remembered, now, that he had fallen asleep and awakened, thinking the telephone had wakened him, and reached for it and heard only the dial tone. Then he must have fallen asleep again, or asleep enough to dream.

Now, because he had, he felt an almost unbearable guilt. He felt that he had betrayed Pam and that the betrayal was irretrievable, and this conviction became a heavy shadow in which he moved. Logic would not lighten this shadow and, indeed, his mind made little attempt at logic. He stood up, abruptly. He leaned over the telephone, and dialed a number and got a heavy voice in answer, a tired voice.

"He's on the phone," the voice said. "You want to hold on?"

"Has he heard anything?" Jerry asked, and the voice said, "Not that I've heard, Mr. North. He'll call you. Or do you want to wait?"

There was no point to waiting; there had been no point to calling. That Bill Weigand was doing what he could, with men all over the city helping, did not need to be said; he did not need to telephone to find it out. That, when anything was discovered, he would be told was as obvious.

"I'm going out," Jerry said. "I'll call him."

Until he said it, until he replaced the telephone in its cradle, Jerry North had not known he was going out. Even now he was not certain where, when he left the apartment, he would go. But he could not stay there longer and wait – merely wait. Pam's mine, he heard his mind saying. She's mine. I've got to find her. It's my job. Pam's mine.

He was in the dark street before he knew what his plan was. He looked for a taxicab then, and found the streets empty. He began to walk, walking north, and as he walked he quickened his steps until he was almost running.

They had not thought of that. They had assumed – at any rate, he had assumed – that whoever had got Pam at the office when she had been playing the record had got the record too. But perhaps he had not. Perhaps Pam had had warning; had had a moment. Pam was quick. She might have hidden the record.

His mind hurried, now, as his body did. If she had managed to hide the record, a good deal would be explained. If she had merely heard it, if whatever story it told was by now in her mind only, the record destroyed, then –

173

then she would not be alive. But if the record still existed, and only she knew where it was hidden, then she might be kept alive until –

And she was alive. She had to be. And – a few hours before, she almost certainly had been, unless Lyster was lying, unless –

She was alive because she had to be. *Had* to be. She was alive because the story on the record still existed; existed in a voice, or more than one voice, and in the grooves of a plastic disc.

It had started at the office; Pam's part in it had started there. At the office he would find –

"Yes," Bill said. "I realized he would be. I'm very sorry. It is important, Mrs. Osman."

"I don't know," the woman – a young woman by her voice's sound – said. "I really don't know, Mr. –"

"Weigand," Bill said, for the third time. "Captain Weigand. Of the Homicide Squad. In New York. Please tell your husband –"

"All right," a man's voice said. "All right, Amy. I'll –"

"He says he's the police," the woman said. "Something about Homicide."

It had taken time to get an answer from the residence of J. Bradley Osman, on Mercer Street, in Princeton, New Jersey. Mr. and

Mrs. Osman had played bridge late that night; they slept soundly. It was taking more time to wake them up.

"All *right*, Amy," Osman said. "All *right*." It was evident that he had come in on an extension. "I'll —"

There was a disturbance on the line. " — trying to get —" an operator said. "Hello," Osman said. "You still there? What's this about homicide?"

"You're Miss Hilda Godwin's agent?" Bill asked.

"Sure," Osman said. "Don't tell me she's got mixed up in homicide. Just when —"

"Miss Godwin's been killed," Bill said, and waited until Osman swore, in incredulity, in apparent shock. He listened further; he said he was trying to find out.

"I need help," he said. "You were handling a novel she'd written. Something she called, 'Come Up Smiling'?"

"Yes," Osman said. "What's that got —"

"Have you got a copy of it?" Bill asked. "A copy of the manuscript?"

Osman said he didn't get it. Bill was patient. He explained briefly. The book might give them a lead. They had been unable to find a copy.

"The Hudson Press has one," Osman said.

The Hudson Press hadn't. Bill explained again.

"Lost it?" Osman said. His voice was even more shocked, it seemed to Bill Weigand, than it had been when the agent learned of his client's death. "Lost the *manuscript?*" Osman seemed incredulous, as well as shocked.

"I'm afraid so," Bill said, still patient. "Have you got a copy? I suppose you have."

"No," Osman said. "She only sent one. I sent it along to the publisher. She's going –" He stopped. He swore, more briefly. "She was going to send me another copy. Wanted me to try the magazines, although I don't know whether –" He stopped. "Why don't you look around and find one of hers?" Osman asked. "I'd think that would be simpler –"

"We have," Bill said. "Through her house in town. Her house in the country. We haven't found a copy."

They hadn't looked, Osman said. That was the trouble, they hadn't looked. They didn't know authors.

"Never knew an author to throw anything away," he said. "Anything they'd written, I mean. First draft, revision, second draft, third draft. Three, maybe four, copies from a typist. They keep 'em *all.* Keep piles of them. Never knew one who didn't. There's something sacred about a manuscript, you'd think. You'll find half a dozen."

"We haven't," Bill said. "I assure you, Mr.

176

Osman. You really mean half a dozen?"

Osman hesitated a moment.

"Probably," he said. "She's been —" He corrected the tense again. "She'd worked on this thing for a couple of years. Told me she'd done two drafts and settled for the second. Two complete drafts, I mean. Part of it she typed herself; recently she's been trying this gadget. Dictating machine thing, you know."

"Yes," Bill Weigand said. "I know."

"So she'd have a ribbon copy of each version," Osman said. "And a carbon, probably. Then she'd have — well, she ought to have left anyway two carbons of the final draft. After she'd had it copied, I mean. It had been copied. Nice clean script. So that makes —" He paused to count. "Six anyway," he said. "Not counting the one you say the publisher's lost. Must say that doesn't happen often. Kick 'em around, fuss around with them, take months. Yes. Lose them. No."

"This one they did, apparently," Bill told him. "And, as I said, we can't find any other copies."

"Got to," Osman said. He was awake enough now. "Somebody's got to. My God. A great book. A *great* book. Could be Book of the Month. My God, man, we've *got* to find it."

Bill hoped they would. Meanwhile — could Mr. Osman tell him something about the book?

177

"A great book," Osman said. "Could be —"

"I've gathered it was autobiographical," Bill said. "To some extent, at any rate. Did you think that? You've read it, evidently."

"Well," Osman said. He sounded wary. "Not what they usually mean when they say that, Captain. A lot more than that. Good story, beautiful style. Moving and funny too, sometimes. I wouldn't want to say it was auto-biographical. Not in the usual sense."

"Mr. Osman," Bill Weigand said. Now the patience was very evident in his voice. "Listen, Mr. Osman. I'm not a publisher. Nor a critic. I'm just a policeman. Say it's the greatest book anybody ever —"

"Now," Osman said, "I didn't say that."

"What I want to know," Bill said, "is — did she get most of the material from her own life? Is it, basically, about herself? About people she's met? Maybe been in love with? You know what I mean."

"Well," Osman said. "Yes, I suppose so. Most novels are, you know. First novels particularly. Where else does a writer go for the stuff he uses? Make up plots, sure. Make up people — not entirely. How can they? Sometimes they take a little piece of somebody here and another little piece of somebody there. Come up with Mr. Jones. Mrs. — Zilch."

"Sometimes," Bill said, "don't they more or

less take characters whole? Disguise them a little; give them different professions, describe them differently? Particularly when the book's partly autobiographical."

"Well," Osman said, "yes. I suppose so."

"And – Miss Godwin did that? In 'Come Up Smiling'?"

"Well," Osman said, "maybe."

He was told that he must see what Weigand was getting at. A writer is killed. Simultaneously, all the copies of a novel she had just finished disappear. The novel was, to some extent, autobiographical. It described people who might be alive. Perhaps –

"Well," Osman said, "I do see what you mean. Knew a woman once – perfectly nice gal, far's I could see – that happened to. Married a writer, had a quarrel with him. His next book – whew! Ran into him at a restaurant, somewhere, this gal did and spit in his face. Actually. Give you my word. Can't say I blame her much, either. Of course – spitting. Still – all her life, probably, people'll be saying 'Mrs. Whatever-her-name-is? Oh – weren't you the one who –?' Then they'll stop and look embarrassed and –"

"Right," Bill said. "That's what I mean. I've been told the book was innocuous but –"

"Innocuous hell," Osman said. "It's a great

book. I keep telling you that. What damn fool —"

"From this point of view," Weigand said. "It wasn't meant as a reflection on the book. Or, I don't think it was. A man named Wilson — Bernard Wilson."

"Oh," Osman said. "Well —"

"You know Wilson?"

"Who he is, sure," Osman said. "Maybe met him once or twice. I meet a lot of people. He like the book? Read it for the Hudson Press?"

"He seemed to, very much," Bill said. "He did read it for the publishers."

"Swell," Osman said. "Good man, Wilson."

"You'd agree it's innocuous, then?" Bill asked him. "From this point of view, I mean."

Now Osman hesitated; very evidently hesitated. Then he said, "I'm thinking." Then he said, "To be honest, I wouldn't say there weren't some barbs in it. One man, particularly. Seems the heroine had been in love with this chap and he — well, say he turned out to be a heel. I asked her about that. Told her, I hope this character of hers wouldn't be recognized by a lot of people. By himself, particularly. People can sue about things like that, you know. Don't very often, but still —" Bill Weigand could see a man shrugging in Princeton.

"Well," Osman said then, "she said he was a composite, of course. They always say that. I said, better put a disclaimer of reference in it. You know, one of those resemblance-is-purely-coincidental things. They've been known to help. Shows you mean well, I guess, or are ready to pretend – "

"You didn't recognize this character?" Bill asked him. "Remind you of anybody you know? Or know of?"

"No," Osman said.

"It could be important," Bill told him.

Osman said he realized that. He said he had not recognized the "heel" of Hilda Godwin's book.

"No," Osman said. "Nobody I knew. Off hand, anyway." He paused. "I'll tell you," he said, "this guy was hell with women, chiefly, I gathered. One of the points was that men didn't tumble to him. Know what I mean? General idea, men were too stupid to see that he was really – well, a man who was all front and no inside. Somewhere in the book this gal – the gal the book's about, I mean – calls him a 'façade man.' One of the 'façade men.' "

"No other occupation?" Bill said.

No occupation, Osman said. The man – assuming he had ever existed – might be anything.

"Right," Bill said. "Publisher. Art dealer. Professor. Another writer."

"Could be," Osman agreed. He was thanked.

181

"For God's sake," Osman said, "find a copy of that book. It's a great book. Could be Book of —"

"We'll try," Bill said. "Thanks again, Mr. Osman."

The clock on the dash told her it was ten minutes of six. It was still dark. Clouds which, miles away, had been lace, wind-tossed across a moon, were dark over New York. She drove the station wagon down the ramp, swung it, in Fortieth Street, toward the east. She drove slowly through the almost empty streets. She waited for a light at Madison, turned south for a few blocks, turned east again and stopped at the right hand curb. This block was empty; the buildings along it were blank-faced, their eyes closed against the reluctantly beginning day. Pam switched off the lights of the station wagon, switched off the ignition.

She slid across the seat and opened the door of the car. She felt mentally and physically numb, yet beneath the numbness, was conscious of it, perceived the dullness of her mind and of her movements. She sat for a moment before she stepped from the car and, for that moment, could hardly remember where she was or why she had come there. But then she thought, I've got to get it, and slid from the seat to the sidewalk. She crossed to the building's double doors, and put a finger on the night bell.

She could hear the bell ringing, but it was unanswered. She continued to press the bell for some time before she tried the doors and found them unlocked. Vaguely, she thought the building must open earlier than she had supposed. She went across the small, deserted lobby to the elevators and waited. She rang and waited. When nothing happened she turned away and walked to the stairs. She passed the empty table at which Sven Helder sat of evenings. A light was burning over it. She went up the stairs, slowly and heavily — a small, toiling figure, bright hair streaked and face grimed, in a woolen dress dirtier than either face or hair; with stockings shredded on legs laced with scratches. One of the scratches started to bleed anew as Pam climbed the stairs, but she did not feel the sting. I've got to get it, she said to herself. I've got to find it.

She reached the fourth floor and went along the corridor to the office doors. "North Books, Inc.," was painted black on a ground glass panel. She hesitated. Beyond the panel she could see no light. She tried the door and it opened, and this should have surprised her but did not. (She had not thought the door might be locked; did not feel now that it should be.) She stepped into the darkness of the offices and reached for the light switch at the side of the door. But then she stopped her hand. Light had always been friendly in Pam North's life; now darkness seemed a shelter. She did not attempt to think this out. She stood inside the door for a moment and her eyes adjusted themselves to the light. It was not wholly dark in the office; the windows at the far end, facing on the street, were faintly luminous.

Pam moved among the ordered desks, careful to make no sound. After she had taken a few steps, she stood by a desk, steadied herself against it — but still swayed a little from her utter weariness — and toed off her shoes. She left them where they lay and went on, more quietly.

Her goal was the desk at the far end of the long room. More precisely, her goal was a low shelf behind the desk. On the shelf, as she finished transcribing from them, Miss Corning put records which had served their purposes, spoken their pieces. Monday night the shelf had been almost full; Pam did not know how many records her hurrying fingers had found there, but there had been many.

A book is well hidden in a library; a record in a shelf of records. Pam, in the few moments allowed her Monday night, had slipped the record which told of murder in the middle of the second of three neat piles of records on the shelf. Within a segment of, at most, five of the thin discs her fingers would find it. For assurance, she would take as many from the center of the pile as she could grasp between thumb and fingers.

She reached Miss Corning's desk, steadied herself for a moment, went around it and reached down to the shelf. As she bent forward she almost lost her balance; carefully, then, she crouched in front of the shelf, between it and the desk. She felt for the center pile.

Her fingers found nothing.

She used both hands; her hands, like those of a blinded person, flickered over the shelf. It was empty.

Pam, sitting on her heels, held fast to the shelf. She tried, now, to steady her mind as well as her body.

Had she forgotten where she put the record? Were the three neat stacks of records something which, in the long time of her flight, in the confusion of her flight, she had imagined there? For a moment, in her exhaustion, now in this incomprehensible defeat, Pam lost confidence in her own mind. She regained it slowly, holding to the shelf for balance which had become precarious.

She had put the record there, with the others. It was not there now, nor were the others. But she had put it there.

185

She stood up, slowly. She turned to the desk. The top of the desk was bare. She pulled at the drawers, and found them locked.

As she stood now, she faced the door to Jerry's private office. The door was closed. But now, behind it, through the panel of translucent glass, she saw a dim light. She did not think it had been there when she entered, but she could not be sure. It was faint through the glass; puzzlingly faint.

Pam left the support of the desk. She moved, very slowly, very cautiously, toward the lighted door. She breathed lightly, as soundlessly as she could.

She did not open the door. She got as close to it as she could, and listened with all the intentness she could summon.

She heard it, then. Faint as the light had been, she heard a voice. It was the voice of only one person; it was without emphasis and very soft. She could not make out the words.

But this voice she knew without question; knew as she knew no other voice.

Jerry was there! His voice spoke — softly, with little pauses, in words she could not distinguish. *Jerry's voice!*

Pam North reached for the knob of the door, then. It was as if a light had been turned on in her mind.

IX

Bill Weigand cradled the telephone and sat and looked at it. Then he looked across the room. He smiled faintly. Sergeant Aloysius Mullins was sitting upright in a straight chair, his posture that of a policeman alert. Nevertheless, Sergeant Mullins was sound asleep.

Bill Weigand's smile faded and he drummed lightly on the desk in front of him.

A "façade man" had been maligned by Hilda Godwin in a book called "Come Up Smiling." Perhaps "maligned" was not the word, since there was nothing now available to show whether the description of the "façade man" had been accurate or unjust. Say merely he had been put in a pillory, fairly or in malice. He had been caught and put on view; he had been jeered at, made ridiculous.

Weigand checked himself. He was building much on little; Osman had said only that the man "turned out to be a heel." Semantics entered in; what did Osman mean by "heel"? How excoriating, actually, had been the por-

187

trait of this "façade man"? What kind of man, however flayed in words, would turn to murder? Would any man?

Bill drummed the table. When you came to that, you couldn't tell. Not most, he supposed. But there was no certainty about the human mind. Take a man who thought well of himself; thought extravagantly well of himself — as intellect; as superior man. Very well, as accomplished lover. Take this man and let him read, and know that given time many will read, that he is a — well, "heel" hardly did it. A worm, say — a small, insignificant, crawling object; a thing from which people turned away or, worse, at which they laughed. Say the woman who fashioned this debasing portrait was one such a man had loved, preened himself before, relied upon for admiration.

You still, Bill thought, required a man of a certain type. A woman Osman knew had, Osman said, behaved — well, say, unpleasantly — under somewhat similar provocation. There is nevertheless a gap between unpleasant behavior and murder — a considerable gap. You needed, in this instance, something close to megalomania; something close enough, probably, to be so diagnosed.

Bill looked at Mullins, hardly seeing him. Mullins slowly inclined to the right — very gradually subsided to the right. He reached a certain point and reverted, quickly, to his erect position. This did not waken him. It would be agreeable, Bill found himself thinking, to close his eyes for a few moments; even to put his arms on the desk and his head on them. Only for a few moments.

He looked away from Mullins. He looked at the opposite wall.

Megalomania was, of course, inherent in the mind of the murderer. It was less obvious in some murderers than in others; now and then a murderer might, quite rationally, believe that murder was not only necessary but altruistic. But in the end, one came to an exaltation of self which was not quite sane. This was true, probably, even in murder committed suddenly, without prior thought, in rage. You took a throat in your hands, perhaps; your hands hated. But, unless at some time you became You, you stopped.

I'm half asleep now, Bill Weigand thought. I'm getting nowhere. Who killed Hilda Godwin? Who snatched Pamela North? And — where is Pam now? He did not like the next question. Is Pam alive?

It was still only guesswork that it was some man who had been pilloried in Hilda Godwin's first, and last, novel. There might be other reasons for the disappearance of the manuscript, and the copies of it. Bill tried to think of several, or even of one. His success was not conspicuous. Very well, then, book and murder were connected.

Then – Hilda had been killed by someone who had read the book. That far, he could get. Hilda was killed by someone who had known her well, probably had been in love with her. Also, by someone who thought well of himself.

Tomorrow, when they could really get to work, they might well find some one as yet unsuspected, even unencountered, who satisfied the requirements. In investigations, the villain did, quite often, make his appearance on, as it were, the last page. Until then, however, he would have to go with those he had.

Item, Bernard Wilson, who had admittedly read the book. He found it "innocuous." (Which might depend on whose ox was gored, of course. Or, he might have lied.) Had he been in love with Hilda? He might have been; it was not in evidence. Did he exalt himself? Bill pondered that. He came up with "maybe."

Item, Gilbert Rogers, who did not admit reading the book. But – would the murderer admit he had? Not, obviously, unless he needed to. Had he been in love with Hilda? Yes, admittedly. Megalomaniac? Hm-m. At any rate, by Garrett Shaw's account (unverified), Rogers was violent. Admittedly, if he thought Shaw responsible for what had been in the trunk, he had grounds for violence. But had he?

Item, Garrett Shaw, who had "asked the lady" and accepted her declination. (Not according to Rogers, however.) Had he read the book? There was nothing to indicate he had; nothing to indicate he had not. Hilda might well have given him a copy to read. Megalomania? It hadn't showed, particularly. It might be there.

Item, Alec Lyster. He had, if their information was more than talk at a bar, been much with Hilda a short time before – before Madeleine Barclay. He might have read the book. Self-exaltation? Again, hm-m. The point was, quite simply, that one could tell – not at once, anyway. In time, perhaps, he –

The telephone rang, harsh, insistent. Mullins said, "Hey? What? I'm –" and stopped, coming awake. Bill answered the telephone. He listened. He said, "Right."

"Come on," he told Mullins. "The station wagon's parked outside Jerry's office building."

"Huh?" Mullins said.

"The Godwin car," Bill said. "Wake up, for God's sake!"

"O.K., Loot," Mullins said.

They started for the door. With his hand on the knob, Bill Weigand stopped. His movement was quick as he turned back to his desk, picked up the telephone. He asked for a familiar number.

Bill listened to the signal which meant that a bell was ringing, rhythmically, in the Norths' apartment. He waited until there was no longer any use in waiting; he waited longer than that.

"Could be he's asleep," Mullins said, from the doorway. But he did not speak with conviction. Bill Weigand took the trouble to shake his head. He stood for a moment irresolute, his right hand on the telephone in its cradle.

"We'll stop by there," he said, then. "Come on."

But the telephone bell stopped them again. Bill swore; he returned; he said, "Weigand speaking," and listened. He swore again. He said, "All right, wait there."

"Shaw hasn't showed up again," he told Mullins. "That was Snyder, waiting at the apartment house."

"He hasn't had much time to get there," Mullins pointed out and Bill, after a moment, nodded. The telephone rang again; again Weigand listened.

"Right," he said. "Keep them at it."

Lyster had not appeared at his apartment. Gilbert Rogers had not been found. Neither had Professor Bernard Wilson. Bill stood for a moment; then dialed the switchboard and asked for a Westchester number. He talked, briefly, to a man he called "Captain." He said,

"Thanks, Merton," at the end, and then held the receiver a little way from his ear, and half smiled. He put it back. He said, "Sorry, Captain."

The State Police, in the person of Captain Heimrich — who hated his first name; who was now in charge — reported that Lyster had not returned to his cabin; that Wilson still was missing from his house near the rambling dwelling which had been Hilda Godwin's.

"Let's go," Bill Weigand said. This time they went.

Jerry North turned from Madison into the numbered street, walking east. The street was deserted, the buildings on either side blank faced. He came to the door of the building he sought and pressed the night bell. There was no response. He tried the door, and it opened. Jerry looked at the turning knob in his hand at first in dull surprise, then in growing excitement. The building was locked until eight; it was in charge of Sven Helder until eight, and admittance was under his supervision. Looking through the glass of the door, Jerry saw Helder's table empty, a light burning over it.

He spoke as he went in, and was unanswered. His voice, not raised, was amplified by the marble walls of the small lobby; it seemed to him as if he had shouted Helder's name. He walked across the lobby to the elevators and rang and waited.

He was about to turn away toward the stairs when he noticed that the door of one of the elevators was not quite closed. There was room to get his fingers between door edge and frame. He pulled and the door slid open.

The elevator was level with the sill. On the floor of the elevator, in the darkness, someone lay, doubled up, motionless. Jerry was suddenly cold, but he moved quickly. His fingers found a switch and light poured from the elevator's dome light.

It wasn't Pam. Sven Helder lay on the floor of the car. There was blood on the side of his head and he was breathing harshly; the little room the elevator made was filled with the sound of his breathing.

Jerry crouched beside him, felt for the pulse. It took him time to find the pulse, because he found his hand was shaking. When he did find it, the pulse seemed strong enough.

Touched by Jerry's fingers, Sven Helder opened his eyes. He turned to lie on his back, his knees still drawn up. Then he straightened his legs and lay flat. He looked up at Jerry blankly, and began to speak, not in English. He looked much older than Jerry had ever seen him; the eyes, with the glasses missing, seemed smaller. They were deep sunken.

"Helder!" Jerry said. "Helder! What happened?"

"Don't hit," Helder said. "What do you want? Don't hit."

Jerry got water from a drinking fountain in the lobby. He bathed Helder's face, gently, using a handkerchief. He told Helder to take it easy; he told Helder, not knowing whether it was true, that he'd be all right.

"Who are you?" Helder asked him. "What do you want?"

"You know me," Jerry said. "North. North Books. Who hit you? When?"

Helder closed his eyes. In spite of his fear for the old man, his sympathy, Jerry wanted to shake words out of him. Instead, he moistened the handkerchief again, bathed the battered head again, spoke gently.

"You'll be all right," Jerry said. "What happened? I'll get you a doctor. Tell me what happened."

There wasn't time for this; there wasn't time for anything.

Sven Helder opened his eyes.

"You're Mr. North," he said. "That's who you are. Why did you hit me?"

"No," Jerry said. "I didn't hit you, Mr. Helder."

"At the door," Helder said. "He wanted to come in. He said — it wasn't you."

"No," Jerry said.

"A tall man," Helder said. "Said he worked for Hendriks. Hendriks, you know."

It was another tenant of the building. "Yes," Jerry said.

"Opened the door," Helder said. "Hit me with something."

"He was coming in?" Jerry said. "You let him in?"

"A big man," Helder said. "He wanted to come in. He works for Hendriks. Keys."

"Keys?" Jerry repeated.

The old man made vague gestures, as if he was trying to reach into a pocket.

"Your keys," Jerry said. "Here." He felt Helder's trouser pockets; the single pocket of the sagging sweater. The pockets were empty.

"He got the keys," Helder said. "Hit me on the head."

The sunken eyes closed again.

It was taking time; there wasn't any time. But the old man's face was gray in the harsh light from above; his breathing remained stertorous. Jerry couldn't leave him there, unaided.

He crossed the lobby with long strides. In a telephone booth, he searched his pockets for a coin. Finally he found a quarter. Every movement took uncountable time, irretrievable time. Finally the operator answered.

An ambulance was needed. Jerry told her

where. It would bring the police, too. Sometime — sometime. There wasn't that
much time, Jerry's nerves told him. He made
himself speak slowly, distinctly; explain that it
was an emergency. He gave his name. Finally,
he could hang up.

Helder was breathing as before. His eyes were
open again. He was looking up at the light.

Pam — *Pam!* — had taken a first aid course
once; he had helped her. Amateurs shouldn't
move the injured; amateurs, meaning well,
might kill.

Jerry left Helder on the floor of the elevator,
staring up at the light. Jerry North went up the
stairs.

As she pulled the door toward her, Jerry's
name was on Pam's lips. It would have been
spoken in eagerness, in unmeasurable relief.
But it was not spoken.

The voice continued, only for seconds, but
for long enough. "Page 97," the voice said, "try
to get him to clean up long passage beginning
—" The voice ended. But before it ended, Pam
had known: had had time to check the word she
was about to speak so gladly; to have exhilara-
tion snuff out in her mind as the voice snuffed
out. It had been from the Voice-Scriber, of
course. It had always been there — a thin,
distant voice; a thin wire of voice. Jerry himself

197

was – Jerry was three thousand miles away.

The room had been dim, except for the surface of the desk. An adjustable fluorescent light made the desk top bright. But now – and this happened not in sequence to the stopping of the voice, but simultaneously with it – the light rose to glare into her face, leaving everything behind it dark. For an instant, Pam saw the hand which turned the light up and toward her. It was a man's hand.

The whisper came from behind the light. It was harsher than before, as if the speaker now found a whisper difficult to sustain. It seemed to Pam that there was a new violence in the sound, although the words were not violent.

"Well, here we are again," the man said. "Back where we started."

"Again" to rhyme with "rain." To rhyme with "pain." But what Pam felt was too dull for pain, too hopeless. She said nothing; she raised her hands to shield her eyes from the light.

"You got out," the man said. "How did you manage that?"

She did not answer; she shook her head hopelessly.

"Don't be stubborn," the man said. "I don't like stubborn women. How did you get out?"

"There was a trap door to the attic," Pam said. Her voice was as dull as her mind, as without inflection. "There was a window. The roof."

"Enterprising," the man said. "Stubborn and enterprising. A waste of time, wasn't it? All you went through." He paused; she could feel him looking at her. "A good bit, apparently," he said. "You look it. And ran in a circle."

He laughed, then. Even the harsh whisper was more gentle than the brief laughter.

"To tell me where you hid it," he said. "You run back in a circle to tell me. Through thorns, apparently."

Dully, she thought, he's enjoying this. Behind the light, faceless — in power. Like an evil god, enjoying what he does.

"Where is it?" he said. "What did you do with it?"

Why was he doing this? He had the record; obviously he had it. He had taken the stacks of records from the shelf behind Miss Corning's desk. He was playing them one by one, seeking the record he wanted. It was only a matter of time. He must —

But perhaps he did not know! Of course — he could not really know. He was right, or would be right. But he could not be sure of that. A matter of time — and no murderer has enough time.

"I asked you a question," he said, and now, oddly, there was a querulous note in his voice. "I expect an answer," he said. He was, Pam thought, almost aggrieved.

She shook her head.

"Oh yes," he said. "This time, you'll tell me. See?"

The hand came momentarily into the light. The hand held a revolver. The hand and the weapon went back into the darkness behind the light.

"Where is it?"

Now, for the first time, he abandoned the whisper. He spoke in a low voice; a low, heavy voice.

The voice of the record? It must be, of course. Pam's mind turned on itself, sought back into itself. She tried, desperately, to remember. But her mind was too tired; too numb. The quality of that voice on the record — what was it? Was this it? It had to be. But — but this voice, even as she heard it, made no impression on the dulled surface of her mind. She could not hold anything in her mind.

Anything but fear — the crude, unmodulated fear of the animal. The fear a bird feels, without thought, in the mouth of a cat — a fear so intense a bird may die of it, and of it only. She felt the body's fear, which numbs the mind, her mind too tired to reject it.

Because — *he did not hide his voice in a whisper now!*

There could be only one reason. Whatever

she did, whatever she said, she was going to die. He had decided that.

"It isn't here," he said then, still in the low, heavy voice. "I thought it might be one of these." He did not show her what he meant. "In the desk," he said. "It would have been a good place. One record with half a dozen. Temporarily a good place. But it isn't here. Where is it?"

He gave her time. She had been numb with weariness; too numb to fight against fear. But he gave her time. Pam North's mind, with a resilience seemingly of its own, beyond her will, struggled through numbness.

He hadn't found it. He had been wrong. Then — *she had a chance!*

"You can't kill me until you know, can you?" she said. "You have to find it first. Why should I tell you?"

"Oh," he said, "to stay alive."

She shook her head.

"You'll have to," she said. "Find the record first. Destroy it." Her mind was quick, now; the numbness quite gone. "Because it identifies you."

"The voice," the man said. "Only the voice. I've been going back over it. She didn't —" He stopped suddenly. "This does no good," he said. "Where is it?"

"Whatever the record says," Pam told him. "Maybe you don't remember right. Maybe it isn't only the voice. You have to know, don't you?"

"I'll know," he said. "You'll tell me. To live."

"No," Pam said. "I wouldn't live, would I? Because I heard it. I remember."

"The record's a fact," he said. "What you remember —" She could feel a shrug. "One woman's memory," he said. "Against the word of —" He broke off. "Against my word," he said. "I'll chance that. I'll —"

"Why should —" Pam began.

"Be quiet!" he said. Now he whispered again. "Somebody's coming. Don't move."

He moved himself. She could hear him. He turned the chair behind the desk, and the swivel squeaked faintly. (I'll have to tell Jerry the chair squeaks, Pam North thought. Tell him — Oh, Jerry! *Jerry!*) There was the faint sound of movement beyond the desk.

"Turn the other lights on when I say," the whisper said. "Get rid of whoever it is. Tell whatever story you — think is safe. Only, get rid of whoever it is. Probably that janitor chap, come to."

"You —" Pam began.

"Keep your voice down," the man whispered. "In the washroom. With the door not closed. Not quite closed. So you'd — *now!*"

Pam reached behind her and touched a light switch. An overhead light came on. The famil-

202

iar office was now as it always was — almost as it always was. She straightened the desk lamp, so that light from it flowed to the desk top.

The door of the washroom was partly open. For an instant, a hand showed in the opening. The hand held the revolver. The hand and the revolver disappeared; the door remained a little open.

Pam North turned and faced the door leading to the outer office. As she turned, lights went on in the outer office. She heard someone walking there, coming nearer. Through the ground glass of the door she could not see who was approaching. The footsteps sounded heavy on the tile of the office floor.

She recognized the steps, then. She wanted to scream a warning.

"Don't try it," the whisper said. "Tell whoever it is that everything's all right."

She could only wait — wait while the steps she knew came nearer the door, wait for the sound of the knob turning. She stood between the desk and the door, facing the door. She waited for the door to open. It seemed to take an infinite time in its slow opening.

Jerry stood in the open door. His face was lined as she had never seen it. His eyes were incredibly tired.

She waited only an instant. She watched, in that instant, the utter change in the eyes — the dear eyes! — in the whole face, as Jerry saw her standing there. She saw that he was about to speak.

"Yes?" Pam said then. "I'm afraid the office isn't open yet. If you wanted to see Mr. North. He's — I'm afraid he's out of town, anyway. If you will —"

She heard her voice going on. She saw Jerry's face change again. *Understand!* she told him, without words, her mind driving at his. *Understand!*

"Just making the rounds, lady," Jerry said. "Saw you had a light on in here. Figured it was pretty early is all. Thought I'd better check and —"

"Come in, Mr. North," the whisper said from the door of the washroom. "Come in and join your wife. Perhaps you can persuade her, you know."

The hand with the revolver in it appeared in the door opening.

Jerry hesitated for an instant. Then he stepped forward. And then Pam went into his arms.

"Very touching," the whispering man said. "Tell him what I want to know, Mrs. North."

The revolver seemed to nod at them.

They had stopped by the Norths' apartment, using to enter it a key which had come into the possession of the Weigands once when, the Norths away, Dorian had acted as a cat sitter. They found three cats, no humans. The cats watched while Bill Weigand wrote a note, "Gone to your office. May need you there," and left it where Jerry would see it when he returned — on the desk in his study.

There was a typescript on the desk, neat in a gray binder, with an envelope inserted in it to mark the place. The typescript of a full-length book, Bill judged from its bulk, looking at it absently. About the size, probably, of the script of Hilda Godwin's novel — of the novel which, found and read, might tell them all they needed to know; the novel which, if a murderer could prevent it, they were not going to find or read. A novel which had, almost certainly, been destroyed.

As he thought that, turning away, words echoed in his mind — words J. Bradley Osman, literary agent, had used, among so many others. "There's something sacred about a manuscript, you'd think."

To a writer, Osman had meant. The sanctity, he had indicated, appertained primarily to the manuscript of an author's own composition. Bill stopped suddenly. Had Osman meant that? Or, casually, had he implied more — that, to a writer, there is something especially to be prized about any manuscript, even one of somebody else's fashioning?

It could be true, Bill thought. It could be that, to a writer, a typescript, almost distinct from the matter it conveyed, might seem to have a special value. Among the intangibles with which a writer dealt, the physical manuscript might come to seem something tangible and immediate; more immediate even than the printed book. Perhaps a writer might hesitate to destroy, to blot out, even another writer's typed pages. Through his association with Jerry North, Bill had met a few writers. There were few among the human vagaries he would put beyond them.

And, now that he thought of it, there was another thing, perhaps less fanciful. Suppose a man to have special interest in literature – as a practitioner of it, or merely as a reader. Or as a collector, say. Would such a person perhaps hesitate to destroy, irretrievably, a work he thought good, even if he would go to the extent of murder to prevent its publication? Would a critic, or another writer or, when one came to that, a publisher or a collector (which Shaw might readily be) not think a good book more to be prized, and preserved, than the author of the book? Suppose "Come Up Smiling" was as good as Osman said it was, or almost as good, would not Wilson, say, find the killing of it more difficult than the killing of a person?

It was worth looking into. Bill picked up the telephone on Jerry's desk and called the office in West Twentieth Street. The State Police were to be communicated with. Requests were to be made. The searches were to be thorough.

Sergeant Mullins listened and was doubtful. You went to a lot of trouble — which murder was, after all — to prevent the publication of a book (not that that in itself wasn't screwy enough!) and then, with your hands on the book, you didn't destroy it? Maybe the Loot knew best. In recent years — since the long ago day when a cat's footprint and the taste of lobster had guided to the solution of a case — they had met a good many screwy people. Mullins waited, without comment.

They went, then, expeditiously enough but in no great haste. The station wagon, having been located, was being watched. It would not be permitted to depart without authorization. Anybody who tried to depart in it would be held. Until then, enough rope was to be given.

Bill Weigand was reasonably confident he knew what the man who had arrived in the station wagon was up to. He was also, although not to the same degree, confident he knew who the man was. Granting the validity of his whole chain of reasoning — which he had to, provisionally — there was one man who fitted better than any of the others.

But he was not prepared to find Helder lying on the floor of one of the two elevators, breathing heavily, staring fixedly up at the dome light above him. He was not prepared for the little he got of Helder's story before a sergeant and a patrolman arrived in a prowl car and said, "All right, what's going on here?" in hard, suspicious voices. He was not prepared for the ambulance which arrived a few minutes later.

"Quite a bump, but he'll probably do," the ambulance interne said. "All right, Georgie."

They started to pick Helder up on the stretcher. They were asked to wait a minute; to answer a question. Who reported this?

The interne looked at a slip of paper. "Man name of North," he said. "All right, Georgie."

The station wagon remained in the street outside. A precinct man materialized from shadows across the street. Nobody had gone out. Yes, one man had gone in. Yes, the rear exit was under observation. No, the only way from the bottom of the fire escape led through a narrow court which debouched within view of the man on watch in the rear.

"Right," Bill Weigand said. To Mullins he said, in a quiet voice, that perhaps they had better be getting along up. They would, he said, walk. The elevators were very noisy gadgets.

They left the uniformed men in the lobby, to

come if needed. A whistle would tell them if there was need. Bill and Mullins began to climb.

X

Jerry had listened. They stood side by side, Jerry's left arm around Pam, holding her tight to him. They faced the door behind which the whispering man waited, but they could not see him. They could see only the hand which held the revolver. The revolver was steady, now.

The washroom was near a corner of the office. Its door, hinged on the left as they faced it, shut off light which otherwise might have entered it from the room. As a result, with no light burning there, the washroom was in deep shadow. They could, behind the gun, make out only the deeper shadow which was the waiting man.

"Speak so I can hear you," the man whispered across the room. "Tell him where it is."

"I don't know," Pam said. "I keep telling you. It's gone from — from where I put it. You — why do you lie? You must have found it."

"I shall," the man said. "I haven't. Where is it?"

"You're sure it's gone?" Jerry asked,

and Pam said, "Yes."

She was trembling with weariness, and with fear. But it was not so bad as it had been. Jerry's arm helped; his presence helped. "I looked," Pam said.

"Then – tell him," Jerry said.

She hesitated. For so many hours there had been the one thing – not to tell. Whatever he did, not to tell. Because as soon as she told he would have no reason to keep her alive. It was now strangely hard to break down resistance in her mind. Her mind kept saying, "No. Don't tell. Don't ever tell."

"It doesn't make any difference," Jerry said. "If you are sure it isn't there." He looked at the shadow behind the door. "No difference to you, either," he said.

"Nevertheless," the man whispered. "Tell him."

Pam told them both.

"All right," the man said. "Now – you." The revolver pointed at Jerry North. "Where would they be if, as she says, they aren't there now?"

"I don't know," Jerry said. "After they're transcribed, my secretary piles them there until –" He broke off. He looked down at Pam. "You're sure you put this record there?" he said. "You really did?"

"Yes," Pam said.

"Then it's gone," Jerry told them both.

"They're all gone."

"There's no use in that," the man said. "But — go on. What do you mean?"

"They've been sent back to the company that makes them," Jerry said. He spoke slowly. "To the local branch. Every Tuesday Miss Corning has a boy bundle them up — all the ones we've transcribed from, don't want to save — and he takes them back to the Voice-Scriber people. And — they shave them. Whatever they do. Scrape off the sound so that they can be used —"

"You're lying," the man said. "It won't do you any good."

"No," Jerry said. "The words are gone. Wiped off — scraped off — whatever they do. It's all — erased."

Then, unexpectedly, he laughed. He was told, harshly, to be quiet.

"Why?" Jerry said. "Don't you think it's funny? You kidnap my wife. Drag her around the country. Up to South Salem. You —"

"Was that where it was?" Pam said.

"Go on," the man said. "Tell your amusing anecdote, Mr. North."

"Yes," Jerry told Pam. "To South Salem."

"And," Pam said, "the trunk —?"

"A girl named Hilda Godwin," Jerry said. "You remember? She wrote —"

Pam said. "I remember. Little — songs."

"I told you to go on, North," the man said. "What is funny? You talk too much."

"No," Jerry said. "You did that, didn't you?"

His arm was tightening around Pam. He was — almost imperceptibly pushing her toward the left; inching them both toward the left. He had been, she realized now, doing that for a minute or longer; he was talking to spin it out. He was, she supposed, lying about the records to spin it out.

As they moved, the door came more and more between them and the man behind the door. If he opened it much farther — and he seemed, engrossed by what Jerry was saying, to be opening it slowly wider — light would fall on him. But if he did not, and they continued to move, there would be a moment when the door was between him and them.

Jerry laughed again. There was no mirth in it; Pam had never before heard him laugh so.

"Don't laugh," the man said. His voice — he no longer whispered — was almost shrill. "I told you not to laugh. I told you —"

"You've forgotten," Pam said. "You told *her* not to laugh. Before you killed her. Called her a name, and called her a snake and —"

She stopped because Jerry's arm pressed her again; urged her to move with him, inch by inch, slowly. Then Jerry laughed again.

"The sound of your own voice," Jerry said.

"You must have talked a lot. Made a record of murder. She fooled you in the end, didn't she? Turned the machine on when you began to threaten —"

"Stand still," the man said. "Where's the record? You lied about it, of course. Where is it?"

"On the wind," Jerry said. "Scraped off and thrown away. So you made a fool of yourself, didn't you? Made a fool of yourself again. She tricked you and chance tricked you. If you'd kept your mouth shut, first. Then, if you'd done nothing — just waited. But now — you can't get away with it now, can you? The record doesn't matter now."

He laughed again. He urged Pam again toward the left. She could feel the tenseness in his body.

No, Pam's mind said. *Don't. He'll kill you. Don't laugh — he'll kill you!*

He had killed when the girl laughed. When she called him pompous, taunted him.

Don't, Jerry, Pam's mind said. *You don't know!*

"Quite a talker, you must be," Jerry said. "Talked yourself into it, didn't you? The sound of your own voice. And now they've rubbed out the sound you were so afraid of. And now it's too late. Now it doesn't matter. Funny, isn't it?"

He managed to laugh again. The revolver

followed them. It seemed to shake.

"Must leave you feeling pretty impotent," Jerry said.

The man behind the door screamed at them, then. His voice was shrilly high; words — ugly words, violent words — screamed through the office.

And the revolver steadied.

Jerry pushed hard and Pam reeled from him, caught herself against the wall. At the same instant, Jerry bumped for the door.

There was one shot. Its sound seemed to fill the office. Pam's hands sought to hold the smoothness of the slipping wall; she crumpled against the wall; was on the floor.

Jerry's body hit the door. The man must have moved quickly as the door slammed toward him, but he was not quite quick enough. The revolver was caught between door and frame, wedging the door a little open.

Jerry's hand reached for the barrel of the revolver, closed on it. For an instant Pam, her eyes wide, could see him struggle for it, twisting it away. Then the revolver came free in Jerry's hand. He relaxed his pressure on the door for an instant and drew the gun out. He strained to close the door again, throwing the gun aside.

The man inside was pushing against the door. The crack did not narrow. It seemed to

Pam slowly to widen.

She moved, then. It was hard to move; her progress was harrowingly slow. She did not quite get to her feet as she crossed the office. Only at the last instant could she make herself stand erect, lean with Jerry against the door; push with him against the resistance within.

It didn't help much; she was too tired to help much, too slight in body for the force needed. It couldn't help enough.

But it helped. Inch by inch, it helped.

Then, abruptly, resistance ended. The door slammed shut. Jerry's hand dropped to the knob, gripped it so his knuckles whitened.

Pam did not hear his voice. Neither of them could ever decide, afterward, whether he had spoken. But Pam got the straight backed chair he wanted and they wedged it under the knob. He held the knob still; leaned still, with all his weight, against the lockless door. But the trap was closed.

"Get —" he began, and this time he did speak. But he did not need to finish. Men were running in the outer office; the door of Jerry's office banged open and Bill Weigand stood in it, gun ready. Mullins stood behind him.

Explanation was not necessary. And Bill Weigand spoke.

"All right, Wilson," he said. "You may as well give up."

There was no answer from the washroom. For a moment there was no sound. Then there was a sound.

"The window!" Jerry said. "He's —"

It took only seconds to wrench the chair away, to pull open the door they had so laboriously fought closed. But the seconds were too long.

Weigand was in the doorway as it opened. He shouted, "Stop!" and his gun went up. But he did not fire.

Bernard Wilson had got through the window, to the sill outside. He faced to the right, moved his feet so that he could leap along the face of the building; clung for an instant to the top of the opened sash.

Then he leaped.

They could not see his fingers just touch the rail of the fire escape platform outside the office window. They could not see the contorted face; the body twisting in a final, hopeless effort.

But they could hear Wilson scream as he fell.

Pam's hands covered her ears, but they could not shut out the scream. She stood for a moment so, and then blackness circled in around her, circled closer and still closer — She did not know when Jerry caught her.

It was a little before six o'clock. Jerry had

made drinks, put them on a tray. He started to carry the drinks to Pamela North in her bedroom, but Pamela appeared at the living room door. She was pale still; her eyes were smudged in the whiteness of her face; the redness of her lipstick was too sharp against pallor.

"I feel fine now," Pam North said, and swayed slightly in the doorway. "Perfectly all right."

Jerry got her to a chair. She admitted that, sitting, she felt better. After a drink she felt better still; she even, Jerry had to admit to himself, looked better.

Two of the cats sat at Pam's feet and stared up at her, intent, as if to re-familiarize themselves with a face almost forgotten. Martini was less forgiving. She sat at some distance, back to her humans who would be required, in the end, to make their peace; to humans who must be taught that cats are not lightly to be left alone for days; that it is intolerable for humans, finally returned, to shut themselves away from cats and sleep the day away.

"Martini's very mad at us," Pam said. The end of the little cat's tail twitched, but the cat did not turn. "It's over now, Teeney."

It was, or almost. Before they slept, Pam had told Jerry how the record had come, how she had listened, and been caught. She told him of the attic, and of the prat-fall when she dropped from the roof, and of the poison ivy. She examined her legs at that point; found them scratched but without ivy symptoms. It was too soon for that, Jerry told her, consolingly; that would come in time. He made her sleep, then, although he could not persuade her to take Nembutal. "You know I don't take *things*," Pam said, and took aspirin, which is not a thing in the category of "things," and slept. Jerry slept too, awakening at intervals to look at the other bed, to reassure himself of a dear, if rather battered, presence. But they both awoke for cocktails.

Bill Weigand arrived a few minutes after six. He had not slept; his always thin face was drawn. He hesitated to take a drink, pointing out that if he once sat down, once drank, he would, quite probably, never get up again; telling them he was on his way home.

"Wilson's dead," Bill told them. "He died a couple of hours ago. He talked first."

Wilson had admitted killing Hilda Godwin – admitted it in many words, sometimes rambling, sometimes violently denunciatory of the dead girl, sometimes endlessly extenuating of himself. It had not, Bill told them, been pleasant. Wilson had gloated toward the end, as he became less rational; he had told them over and over of the way his hands had felt on Hilda's slim throat, of the way she had struggled. He had, as his life ebbed, relived that climax

219

in it; savored murder.

"It was rather as if he thought he had proved something," Bill told them, and now, finally, he did accept a drink. "I suppose he felt he had. A kind of adequacy."

Wilson had admitted killing the little burglar, but about that he was dispassionate. The man had tried to blackmail him; it was appropriate that the man die. He did not seem to know, or particularly to care, how Harry Eaton had found him.

"We don't either," Bill said. "Presumably, Hilda used Wilson's name at some time. Perhaps when he first came in. Eaton was there, of course. He must have heard the name and remembered it and looked it up in the telephone book."

Eaton had had the record in an envelope, addressed to Mr. North, when he arrived at Wilson's apartment Sunday evening. Money, he told Wilson; money, or the record went to the Norths. "Not to us, for obvious reasons," Bill said. "Money doesn't do much good if you're in Sing Sing for life as a fourth offender."

Eaton told enough of the recorded conversation to convince Wilson. Wilson pretended to agree, asked time to get the money. But he had had no intention of agreeing; he followed him, planning to get the record back. He had not been quick enough; he had bungled.

"He did all along," Pam said.

Bill nodded; he said, "Right."

Eaton, before Wilson killed him, got the envelope in a mail box. Wilson had thought of waiting for the collector from the box; had thought better of that. "The government scares people," Bill said. "More than we do." Wilson had decided to get the record from the Norths; he had telephoned, found them both absent, discovered that Pam would return Monday evening.

"Mr. Mutton," Pam said, suddenly. "There was a Mr. Mutton."

They looked incredulously at Pam North. She explained. "I wonder," she said, "what name he really used? Nobody would call himself Mutton."

Bill shrugged. Wilson had not got around to telling that.

He had gone, after dinner, to the North apartment house and been about ready to go in — apparently planning to use whatever method was necessary to recover the record — when Pam came out.

"You were carrying the record in your hand, apparently," Bill said.

"My purse was full," Pam said. She considered. "I really need a bigger bag," she said. "None of this would have happened if —" She stopped. She said she was sorry.

He had followed Pam, driving Hilda Godwin's station wagon. He had left his own car in the country the week end before, not expecting to use it again until spring. He had followed her to the office.

"The record was becoming a kind of obsession, apparently," Bill said. "He had to get it. Of course, he never knew exactly what was on it."

He had died raving about the record. "They lied," he kept saying, in delirium. "They lied. I'll make them tell me where —"

"By the way," Pam said, "where is it really, Jerry?"

Jerry North looked at her blankly.

"I told you," he said.

Then Pam looked blank. Her eyes, already larger than they should have been, grew larger still.

"It was really true, then?" she said. "What you told him? In the end, there wasn't any record?"

Jerry nodded.

"Except in your mind," he told her. "In your memory. What was on the record, Pam?"

Pam tried to remember. She shook her head.

"It's fuzzy," she said. "He was going to kill her. He called her a snake. He wanted her to give him something, I thought, and she laughed. I remember that more than anything

— the way she laughed. I think she called him pompous once and —" She stopped. "What he said doesn't exist anywhere any more, does it?" Pam said. "All of it was about an echo, and it's died away."

"The voice could have been identified," Jerry said. "That was why he whispered when he talked to you; when, until almost the end, he talked to us."

"I don't know," Pam said. "I suppose so. But — it was a very little voice. I thought he might be British from certain words. But I heard — what was his name? The man at the cabin?" They told her. "Lyster," Pam said. "It could have been his voice, I thought." She turned to Bill, suddenly. "Could you really have proved anything from the record?" she asked.

And Bill Weigand shook his head.

"I doubt it," he said. "I doubt that it could even have been got into evidence. The assistant D.A. thinks not. But — it would have told us where to look for evidence we could get in. Like the shovel."

They waited. He did not immediately continue. He seemed, in fact, about to drop to sleep.

"The shovel," Jerry repeated.

"What?" Bill said. "Oh — yes. The shovel. It was broken, of course. He had been trying to mend it. It was a little thing to —" He broke off. He looked at Pam. "To save a life," Bill said. "Yours, my dear."

"A broken shovel?" Pam said. Then she said, "Oh. That was why?"

"Right," Bill said. "He was digging a grave — a large grave. For Hilda. And, if it came to it, for you, Pam. And, he broke the shovel. He was awkward about physical things. You wouldn't have pushed him back into the closet, got the gun, if he hadn't been. So — he broke the shovel, digging. He took it home to try to mend it. The handle was broken. He was trying to wire it together. We found it — the State Police found it — on a bench in the basement of his house." Bill finished his drink; shook his head when Jerry glanced at the shaker. "He wasn't doing a very good job," Bill said, mildly. "I suppose he was still working on it when we showed up and then, naturally, he had to find out what was going on."

"But," Pam said, "just a broken shovel."

"And," Bill said, "the manuscript, of course. They found that, too. A copy of the first draft; one of the final draft. Probably the last was the one Wilson took from the publisher's after he had returned it for the record. If there were others, he destroyed them. But he couldn't, apparently, bring himself to — wipe out the book entirely." Bill paused again; lighted a cigarette. "After all," Bill said, "he was a —

224

what would you call it, Jerry? – a man of letters."

Jerry nodded. They waited.

"Oh," Bill said, "the book's about Wilson, all right. A wicked, ugly story about a man like Wilson. Very witty, very cruel. He's a lawyer, in the book. He makes love to the girl, who is pretty obviously Hilda herself. It's the story of her finding him out, so that in the end she 'comes up smiling.' We've been finding out more about Wilson, and the character fits him. Plenty of people would have identified this man – she called him Benjamin Watson, just to make it easier. In the first draft, she identified him as a professor and all but named Dyckman. Somebody, I suppose, persuaded her that that went a little too far. She went far enough, without it."

He paused. He finished his drink.

"But still –" Pam said.

"Right," Bill said. "Only a megalomaniac would carry it to murder. Not that anybody wouldn't – well, like to wring her neck. She made her identifiable Benjamin Watson a pompous ass. She also hints that he was a – well, an inadequate one to boot. The gossip columnists would have had fun with it. Probably, in the end, the famous professor, the widely known lecturer and radio figure, would have been laughed out of existence. More specifically, he'd probably have been dropped by Dyckman."

They waited.

"The crux of it, probably," Bill said. "He'd have lost his job – the job the rest hinged on. You see, Hilda was an undergraduate when they first met. It's pretty evident they had a love affair. Well – universities don't much favor faculty members who – seduce pretty young undergraduates. As a matter of fact, they fire them."

" 'Seduce,' " Pam said. "I'd almost forgotten the word." She looked at Bill, with directness.

"Was that how you guessed?" she asked. "You named him, through the door."

"Right," Bill said. "If the rest was right, it was Wilson. Because – he had a specific thing to lose. His whole profession. Lyster didn't; Shaw didn't. People would have laughed at them. They'd have laughed at Rogers – and he's a violent young man and wouldn't have liked it. But, he was, it seemed to me, still in love with Hilda, and sure she was with him. That pretty much let him out. Anyway, laughter doesn't kill."

There was a little pause.

"Oh," Pamela North said, "but I think it does. I really think it did."

They waited for her to continue, but she seemed not to think it necessary. She sipped

226

her drink. Then, holding the glass, she appeared to listen to something. Then she looked at the slim legs extended in front of her. Experimentally, she rubbed the heel of her left slipper against her right ankle.

"Well," said Pamela North, "I've got it, all right. Whether it's time or not." She reached down and scratched the ankle, without pretense. "Life," said Pam North, "is ridiculous."

THORNDIKE-MAGNA hopes you have enjoyed this Large Print book. All our Large Print titles are designed for easy reading, and all our books are made to last. Other Thorndike Press or Magna Print books are available at your library, through selected bookstores, or directly from the publishers. For more information about current and upcoming titles, please call or mail your name and address to:

THORNDIKE PRESS
P.O. Box 159
Thorndike, Maine 04986
(800) 223-6121
(207) 948-2962 (in Maine and Canada call collect)

or in the United Kingdom:

MAGNA PRINT BOOKS
Long Preston, Near Skipton
North Yorkshire,
England BD23 4ND
(07294) 225

There is no obligation, of course.